de-pop

A novel by

Russell H. Ford

Amazon Publishing Center
420 Terry Ave N, Seattle, Washington,
98109, U.S.A

Printed in the United States of America.
ISBN: 978-1-915911-17-9 (paperback)

To my one and only wife:
Mollie

———————————

To my parents, who blessed me with the genetic material to succeed.

To my sisters, who set the bar so very high.

To my extended family, who have endured me.

To my friends, who have encouraged, criticized, and challenged me at every turn.

To the Boy Scouts of America, which helped educate me in the really important things in life.

To the North Thurston School District, Lacey, Washington, where curiosity is encouraged.

To the fire service everywhere, especially in Washington State, and specifically the Lacey, Tenino, Lakebay, Seattle, Chelan County District #1, and Pullman fire departments; to Washington Public Power Supply System (Energy Northwest), the Pierce County Fire Marshal's office, the Chelan County Fire Marshal's office, and all fire service training programs. Only firefighters know the truth about the Red Devil.

To law enforcement everywhere, especially in Washington State, and specifically the Thurston, Whitman, Douglas, Chelan, and Pierce County Sheriff's offices and the Lacey, Pullman, Wenatchee, East Wenatchee, Tenino, and Seattle police departments. The Seattle Police Department's SWAT team and shooting range personnel are also worthy of high praise.

I was told several times that a good writer has a great editor. I was blessed with three: Jessica Cromwell, Glenne Stewart, and Martha Goelzer. Plus there are many people—Jeff; Glenda; Doctors Saint Clair, Card, Ruditzky, and Hoffman; Sara; Steven D. Mace; Dean; Tom; the Paramedics; Kat; Dana; Valerie; Louis; and more—who read and critiqued *de-pop*. *de-pop* got better with each review.

To Andrew Hoffman, who built the website from the peculiar ramblings I inflicted on him.

To the Craft at the Russell City Energy Center in Hayward, California, at the Eastern Alberta Transmission Line in Hanna, Alberta, Canada, and at the Kitimat Modernization Project in Kitimat, British Columbia, Canada, who kept in contact asking about *de-pop*, and to the Bechtel Corporation for employing me in great jobs at those locations.

To the Cabo Cantina, Cabo San Lucas, BCS, Mexico, for letting me camp out in Hemingway fashion in the back dining area with my computer, straw hat, and red bandanna as I wrote, rewrote, and made a thousand corrections. Samir and the staff were curious and helpful at every turn. Try the guacamole!

To Doctors R. Phillips, W. Shields, and J. Haynie, who collectively saved me from going blind.

To WOW Salon in Cabo San Lucas, for pampering me when I fried my brain. And to Jack's, where I met the musician Horacio and Captain Charley!

To David S. Schneider, lawyer, Lacey, Washington, for taking on our unique enterprise.

To David J. Segarra, financial advisor, Las Vegas, and former member of Seattle's SWAT team, for the years of patience and support.

To Ralph Munro, longest serving Washington State Secretary of State, for being a friend since the early 1970's.

To Delta Spirit, Karli, Night Supers, BESH, D&L H, DL, Canadian First Nations, James Burke, PT, Bret and Brett, Lacey Library, Tenino Quarry, CFerris.

To Elliott Wolf, Publisher, Classic Day and Peanut Butter Publishing; wherever we end up, it all started there.

To Amy Vaughn, Soundview Design Studio, for putting it all together, an extremely difficult task considering the general malaise and lassitude of the author.

To Mike Marohn, Senior Vice President at the Marohn Crofts Group at Morgan Stanley, Olympia, Washington, who was my soccer teammate at North Thurston High School and has been my financial advisor for thirty years. If I got there or get there, it was because of you.

To Christopher Conrad for his remarkable photographic skills.

To Tezla and Fuzzy Buddies everywhere.

To Sam and Chris for helping kick off the public side of the roll out.

And a special thanks to Jennie, you bailed me out when I needed it!

Russell H. Ford
West Seattle, Washington
January 2015

Preface

I was driving in Seattle, on a Friday afternoon, on the Fourth of July weekend. So, naturally, I was stuck in traffic. My 1985 Volvo, my most favorite car ever, was capable of hitting well over one hundred miles an hour, and would be as stable as a rock when it did. There I was stuck in traffic, with, by my estimate, a few tens of thousands of people I already did not like.

It was clear that my life was sorely impacted by the overbreeding proclivities of humankind. What I personally did not need was another apartment house in West Seattle. I did not need to pay for another school, for children of any age. I did not need to endure crappy road maintenance because too many people were wearing the roads out right before my eyes. I did not need to stand in a line for anything, ever again.

Someone should do something. And the sooner, the better.

I wrote the above many years ago. In the passing years, it has become evident that there are just too many of us scrambling around on the planet trying to eke out a living. In some areas that suffer from chronic drought and persistent crop failures, the population explosion remains unfettered. We, as negligent human beings, have bought into the notion that "more is merrier," yet nothing could be further from the truth, or a worse reflection on humankind. Some cultures embrace aborting girl fetuses so that they can have strong sons to tend the fields and the machinery. Some religions, for whatever reasons, foster the belief that millions of starving uneducated people are better than healthy, vibrant communities.

Still, there are clouds on the horizon: French sperm motility is down by a noticeable percentage, Japanese population is not currently growing as it once did, school closures due to under-enrollment bring out vicious neighborhood spats with the local boards of education.

We can find trace chemicals in water supplies, in the air, and in the food that have no business being there.

My question now is: Has someone started the process?

The Sister stood looking out over the small courtyard adjacent to the church. Sunlight peeked through the clouds and laid a dappled pattern across the landscape. Spring flowers poked their way skyward through the loam. Birds chirped to the morning sun as they fluttered along the eaves. She quietly rubbed her hands back and forth, back and forth. The arthritis had claimed a considerable part of her ability to use her hands for extended periods of time. Being this far from any major town meant limited access to health care to tend to her condition, and made any medications prohibitively expensive. She suffered quietly during her toils.

The Sister was only fourteen when she heard and felt the calling. It was a happy and sad day as she climbed onto the train and waved farewell to her family. The clouds of coal ash and steam made for an interesting byplay as the train chugged out of the village and into the mountains right at dusk. The train greeted the new sunrise on the level plains east of the Andes.

It seemed fitting to leave at night, as she ended one part of her life, and to begin anew on the morrow. Even at a very young age, she was a gifted pianist. But that was over sixty years ago, so very long ago. She looked at her hands: twisted, inflamed, and painful. For so many years she had played at each and every worship service, funeral, and wedding at her church. In private moments, when her aching hands kept her awake, she sat at the old piano and ran her fingers over the keys, keys she could no longer effectively play. The Sister knew she would have to again confess her pride about her ability long since gone. Now she sometimes soaked her hands in water as hot as she could stand in order to just peck out a few notes for the congregation to follow along with. So many floors had been scrubbed, so many parishioners' graves dug by her when no one else would or could. All had slowly robbed the Sister of her musical skills.

It was even difficult at times to pin together diapers in the orphanage. The periodic civil strife that had claimed so many had also left so many to care for. She often cried herself to sleep when she could hear the mortars falling in the jungle many kilometers away. Every blast increased the probability that a new orphan would appear on the doorstep of the church. Many times she sighed and with a gnarled hand wiped a tear from her face; many times the children were wounded, wrapped in bits of fabric soaked with blood. Sometimes when she opened the door in the morning, her heart sank as she discovered the tiny corpse of a child that had not survived the night.

Still, there had been some beneficial things as of late. The sometimes-generous Americans had finally answered one of her many prayers: a new well had been installed just off the center of the village during the previous summer. The number of children who had died from dehydration caused by diarrhea had dropped dramatically.

Indeed, the reduction in the numbers of both sick children and adults who came to the meager clinic for easily treatable illnesses was truly a blessing. And further, the arrival of the new priest last year after the passing of Father Anacortes was also something to be thankful for. The new priest, Father Sedro, often had sermons on abstinence and reminded the parish about the sins of premarital and extramarital relationships. This message was well received by the entire population, congregants or not. The number of children being taken into the orphanage had dropped by one in January, two in February, and four in March from the year before.

The Sister prepared her brief report, still typing hesitantly on the computer the new priest had brought. She entered her children's names and ages and the dates they had arrived on a form the priest called a "spreadsheet." She typed using her right index finger only, laboriously entering the data keystroke by keystroke. Sometimes, the Sister would add a comment or two at the bottom of the report, mentioning such trivia as the songs of the birds on the roof or the types of flowers in the courtyard. On this day, she included a brief mention highlighting the success of the priest's message on the benefits of fidelity. The Sister hit the "send" button, and in doing so, condemned herself to death.

Her high heels clicked along the rough sidewalk a few blocks off the National Mall. It was in the late fall that she—the head of a trade group representing fifteen of the world's largest corporations—came to the Smith, LLC building in Washington, D.C. She had been there before on other matters that required action. Actions that sometimes ran contrary to the political agendas of most of the world's free-market countries.

She smiled a little at that thought. After all, she represented *business*, and that was far more important than *government*. She and her predecessors had done more to defeat communism than all the saber-rattling flag wavers on Capitol Hill. It was simple—communism was just plain bad for business, and it had to end in order for business to prosper.

She and the others who held her position over the decades had attacked governments, religions, and fanaticism. With measures of malevolence and calculation, they destroyed and built on the premise that if it was bad for business, it was bad for everyone. Everyone who mattered, anyway. Sometimes they took the long view. The work spanned years, sometimes decades. Balance sheets were kept privately. Sometimes change had to take place with alacrity. Sometimes people simply had to die in order for the greater good to be achieved. Generally, if it was good for business, it was good for everyone. Generally.

And it was business that was on her mind today as she was let into the Smith House. It was clear that population was going to increase at an alarming rate, and while that meant more consumers, it was not the consumer class that was worth a damn. Dumb poor people were ultimately not good consumers of computers, smartphones, and tablet PCs. Too many dumb poor people spread diseases, ate all the food, and were never going to aspire to anything more than the next government handout.

What was good for business were people educated to the junior high school level, and not much beyond that. Those people would work hard enough to get a color TV and an internet connection, tools that would show them that a better lifestyle could be had by buying better carpet, a faster computer, a car with a rear-view camera, and more. Much more. If there were too many dumb poor people, government tended to waste the most valuable commodity of all trying to feed them and shelter them, and that commodity was money.

As always, she came with nothing more than her personal memory, a flash drive, and a few bank account numbers written on the back of a business card. One of her early mentors had made a habit of wandering the House and Senate office buildings picking up business cards of people he despised. On these he would write the phone numbers for brothels, sex change clinics, gay and lesbian chat lines, and other scandal fodder before dropping them in restaurants where reporters gathered for coffee. He then would set up Google Alerts and watch the fun flash across his monitor.

The Trade Group, or TG, did not consider governments to be vital to its interests. In reality, the TG had long ago transcended the need for individual governments, as it had embraced globalism long before the League of Nations was even dreamt of. The TG decided who ruled whom and for how long. A brief email joke was passed amongst the TG members showing a collage of the constitutions of several dozen countries, with the caption *"What Fools Believe."*

The corporate world ruled the world. Everything else was just too transient to be of substance. She was motioned into one of the rooms off the main entry of the Smith House. She knew that she had to put her considerable ego on hold for the time she was here. The Smiths—staff, guards, and administrators—all had reputations of shooting first, and often, and were not bothered to ask questions before or after. Here she stood at the desk while a slender gray-haired man of indeterminate age looked her over. He nodded to a chair. No handshake, no informal banter, no off-color jokes, just business, which is what she came to conduct.

"Problem?" the man asked.

"Too many people," she said. He nodded; she nodded.

She passed the flash drive over, and the business card. He put the flash drive in his pocket. The fine tailoring of his suit could not conceal the bulge of a large-frame automatic. He looked at the numbers on the back of the card and noted a familiar phone number for a decidedly decadent bondage club in London's Soho intersperced with the bank account numbers. He flipped the card over and permitted himself a small smile; the head of the soon-to-be-forgotten Tea Party, as well as the Tea Party itself, would be very unhappy to have this card see the light of day in the press. Mr. Smith said "Thank you, we shall be in touch." She rose and walked to the door, high heels accentuating the shape of her calves.

Nice ass, he thought.

Neah Bey's job was to carry out the Will of the United States of America. People who are and will always remain nameless decide the Will of the United States of America. But these people are not faceless or voiceless. Bey knew this because he had spoken to them on several occasions as their employee.

No one told him the work would be easy, the travel fun, or that he would be wined and dined in fine restaurants around the world. Bey discerned the truth of the matter when he was making an incursion into North Korea and had to eat dog. He thought it was dog. It was some hapless roadkill left in a rut in the road.

When you are freezing cold, fifty miles over the border and out of radio contact, dog isn't bad. At least that was what Bey was trying to convince himself. He slowly chewed the partially frozen carcass and figured it was his last meal. Sort of a crappy last meal.

He was a very young priest in South Eastern France when the Nazis came to power. Then, at first, there was much talk of war and what that might mean to the Church. No one considered for a moment the depth of evil that lay just across the Eastern border. He had many friends in the ministry, including some from different faiths. They gathered from time to time to debate religious issues amongst themselves. It was well after the end of the Roaring Twenties and the Depression that had rocked the world. The monsignor said they should look upon troubled times as opportunities to gather more of a flock. In his heart, the priest knew that most were just drawn to the Church for a warm bowl of soup and a crust of bread.

His Jewish friends began to leave in little clumps of extended families. One old friend said he was just going to try to stay out of artillery range so he could come back home quickly when it was all over. Some of the Jewish families stayed. They simply had no relatives anywhere to turn to.

Then one day the Nazis arrived. Not in the blitzkrieg that everyone feared—they just simply showed up and took over. The French Army had already retreated in the night, leaving the priest's small village in no-man's-land. He awoke in the morning to find himself a citizen of Germany. At first things were fairly unchanged; the market was still open, a bottle of wine for dinner could still be purchased at the corner store, and if nothing else, the church was filled almost to bursting the very next Sunday, and thereafter as well.

The local commandant seemed pleasant enough; he tipped his hat whenever he rode by on his rounds of the countryside. Only in the quiet of the night could the distant thunder of artillery be heard and the occasional flash of light seen over a faraway hill. Sometimes planes were seen at high altitude crossing the heavens with their icy contrails.

Then the circumstances, and it seemed the very air the townspeople breathed, began to change. At first the bread was rationed. It was needed to feed the conquering German Army as it advanced across France and northern Italy. A few weeks went by and then half the milk and butter was taken away, again to feed the victorious Germans. A meeting was held in the town square. The commandant stood silently and listened to each and every complaint from the local population. He looked from time to time at a youngish officer next to him to prompt the making of a note of an issue on a large tablet of paper. The commandant was always polite, and encouraged everyone to voice his or her opinions of the current situation. When the people had said enough and the murmurings quieted down, the commandant raised his hand and asked again if there were any more issues that he needed to be made aware of. There were none. He smiled broadly, thanked them all for attending, and said that he wanted to make sure he was leaving everyone with an exact understanding of how the relationship between the victorious German Army and the townspeople would be from then on. With that he drew his sidearm and shot the mayor through the head. Bits of bone and brain showered the crowd. The crowd stood as the mayor's body fell face first on the street. A rivulet of blood flowed between the cobbles. Then the townspeople ran, in all directions. The commandant ordered his men to fire into the air to make sure that those who had stayed home would also get the message: the Germans had taken over, completely.

———————

While he had not voted for either of the candidates in the last presidential election, to some degree he worked more for the president than did the Cabinet. Not directly though. Never directly. There were a series of disconnects between the president and Bey. The president would never know who Neah Bey was. The president would know what Bey had accomplished through messages, emails, briefings, and quickly discarded handwritten notes. The relationship was set up to ensure what's called *plausible deniability*.

If something were to go wrong, and it sometimes had with others like Bey, his employers hoped Bey would have the ability to kill himself so that they could maintain their plausible deniability.

There was a stack of folders located in a deep basement in an obscure building in Washington, D.C., that contained Neah Bey's picture and other personal details. Depending upon where his corpse was found the appropriate folder would be pulled out identifying him as a Baptist, Jew, Muslim, agnostic, atheist, Confucian, Hindu, Buddhist, or some other persuasion.

Every few months, a minor functionary unlocked the elevator and descended into the sub-basement. There he or she would refigure Bey's age, weight, current medications, and recent injuries, and update his picture. The functionary did this for Bey and for one hundred and twenty-five people like him.

Neah Bey did not consider himself to be a zealot, although in the eyes of his detractors he was often confused with one. Bey and his associates, the one hundred and twenty-five others, were not radicals, idiots, or victims of brainwashing. They were simply employees. Employees with skill sets not normally advertised for in the *Wall Street Journal*.

They, the 125, understood that there are things the government must do to preserve its way of life, its method of operation, its *continuity*, that are not necessarily right or wrong. They just are. These are the things that everyone suspects that every major government does, but cannot prove. Taken together, these things comprised the expression of the Will of the United States.

The Will of the United States was not, and would never be, what the two houses of Congress voted on, and it was not something that select committees discussed in open or closed sessions. It was, however, formulated by the powerful, the rich, and the career bureaucrats that pushed the country into wars, out of wars, and away from wars. It was not up for a vote. Indeed the public would have been shocked and amazed to learn that public figures had little to do with crafting the Will of the United States. Politicians were far too fleeting in their careers to be held in trust for much of what the Will had become, or would become.

———

Delano "Del" Omak sat in his nearly silent apartment. The only noise that came in was the occasional traffic rumble, or maybe the distant hum of some building service. Omak's room was sterile, devoid of color, absent of personality. It was cold. Most of the time, Omak felt like his room. Empty and lifeless.

It had not always been that way. Before, there was humor, color, life, and love, and now there were none of those or the other things that humans gather about themselves as artifacts of existence. No paintings or pictures graced the walls, no collection of knickknacks adorned a windowsill, no certificates in nice wood frames hung near the desk. It wasn't really a desk at all. It was a cheap card table scavenged from a dumpster behind a junk shop, with a bent leg, rust on the metal rim, and a tear on the fabric top. Omak had spent nothing on his furnishings; he slept on a discarded yoga mat, and wrapped himself against the chill Omaha winter in blankets handed out at homeless shelters. In less than ten minutes he could pack up and be gone, leaving everything—or leaving nothing, really—behind.

Except for the computer and the small satellite dish that was clamped to the window frame, which were now all that mattered to him. They fed and supported his new life, born of hate, anger, and frustration. And there was the envelope, which was frayed, dog-eared, and tired looking. It sat on Omak's lap. It was stained with tears.

Neah Bey smirked in the cold and wiped frozen tears from his eyelashes and thought, *We get blamed for a lot more than we deserve. On the other hand, we deserve a lot more blame than we get.* Slim solace as the wind knifed through his camouflaged snowsuit.

Bey took out his small night vision monocular and scanned the trails to his left and right. Of himself and the few of the one-twenty-five that he had been introduced to, he had once said, "We all are remarkably forgettable. None of us are too tall, too short, too thin, too fat, or too anything. We could be the background extras in any movie ever made: we are that unremarkable." Neah did share with the one-twenty-five one desire: that their friends and loved ones live out their lives in relative peace and comfort.

If that meant that the head of a drug cartel needed to be killed, then that would happen. If a scientist came up with a way to interfere with spy satellite communications that was contrary to the the needs of the United States, then Neah and his associates would make contact. If the scientist did not accept cash to suppress the invention, then other methods would be employed. Neah's associates could make him wish that he had never taken his first breath of air because they made his last so painful and so protracted.

And quite unlike the Hollywood movie version of a spy, Bey had not owned a tuxedo since he was an Elk. One senator, when pressing the issue in closed session, demanded to know who "they" were. He was shown a single photograph of a tattoo on the iris of an agent's eye. It was called the midnight mark. It was not a lot of fun getting it; Bey grimaced at the memory of receiving his. The senator said, "Jesus, just to be a dead and forgotten hero?"

Bey scanned the trails again. Shivering had long ago

set in, and he had to use both hands to hold the monocular steady. The moonlight skirted around clouds, causing shadows in the scrub brush to shift and dance. Errant splatters of wet snow cascaded here and there. He had taken great precautions to arrive at the rendezvous point several hours ahead of the meeting time, so that he had time to carefully step from one boulder to the next and leave no visible trail of footsteps to give away his whereabouts. Where he was forced to cross open areas bereft of stones he carefully placed his feet under the tangle of shrubs where there was little if any snow.

Even the very best in arctic and Himalayan clothing was not a match for the hours of limited movement that Bey had to endure. He could feel it start in his toes and fingertips, that achy feeling, as the cold began to bite deeply into his body.

Bey lived in the Pacific Northwest with his wife and six cats, in a house with a modest yard and detached garage. Bey had killed others. He assumed he would have to kill again. Bey frowned; he had aided in the destruction of good people in the pursuit of destroying evil. He was proud to be an American. Sometimes he was not proud of the things he had to do. Dante said there were nine levels of hell. Bey assumed he was headed to the lowest so that others could avoid the trip.

He swung around to get his face a little closer to a rock outcropping, for partial shelter from the ice particles that were whipping off the bushes. Out of the corner of his eye he saw a movement that was not part of the ordinary. Bey rolled to his left and felt a searing pain crush his left rib cage. As he rolled he brought up the .45 Auto and fired two quick rounds at a shadow in the scrub. He continued to roll and put the outcropping between him and his assailant.

With one hand on the monocular he scanned downhill towards where he had fired. The night vision showed a human form dressed in a snowsuit very similar to Bey's on hands and knees. The figure slowly slumped forward without sound, coming to rest face down on the snow and ice. Bey knew the North Koreans usually sent two out for a kill. He traced the fading footprints back down the path his would-be killer had taken. Bey grimly smiled. He dropped his right hand and pulled the glove off between his knees. His hand ran into a sticky chilling trail of blood starting just under his left armpit. Eight inches to the right, the slug would have torn through his heart. A partially frozen finger traced the sharp end of a rib fragment sticking out through his skin. "Shit." Neah knew that his chances of survival were fading with each breath.

Bey put his glove back on and switched the heavy .45 back to his shooting hand. Slowly he craned his head around the rock and used the monocular at its greatest magnification. Even the superb Czechoslovakian optics were only a little help in blowing snow. Yet even in this difficult environment, the optics picked up where his two adversaries had split up. One had been coming straight on; the other was travelling uphill to his right. The rock to the right of his head exploded, sending slivers of coarse stone into the side of his face.

He rolled downhill, head over feet in a mad scramble. Each time his left side hit the ground he gasped in pain. "Shit," he said again as he crashed into bushes and boulders. He knew the coppery taste in his mouth was blood coming up his windpipe from his lungs. As a stout-looking shrub came into view, he grabbed it with his left hand, dropping the monocular in the snow. As the shrub took his weight a blinding flash of pain caused him to spasm from head to foot. He could hear the North Korean running down the hill towards him.

Bey rolled up onto his left knee and knelt, bringing the .45 up. His vision was tunneling from the pain. The North Korean made a fatal error— Bey's adversary crossed between some scattered bushes and for a brief moment was silhouetted against the snow behind. The .45 barked twice and the figure went down.

What had started out as a simple "meet and greet" with a potential defector with advanced knowledge of the North Korean missile and biological weapons programs had gone significantly awry. Bey winced as he crushed a "go" pill between his teeth. The sour acid taste on his tongue was unpleasant. He waited a moment to make sure that the second human was down, and then took a painkiller. He began to tremble, and it was all he could do to put the pill into his mouth. Bey chewed the tablet into a pasty mush. A doctor friend had told him, "When in doubt, chew the hell out of it, wash it down, and pray it works fast." Bey grabbed a handful of snow and let it melt in his mouth before swallowing. A coughing fit was somewhat silenced by his gloved hand. Using the nearby snow he attempted to wipe the red spray from the glove.

The gray-haired man in the tailored suit descended the stairs into the basement of Smith, LLC, in Washington, D.C. No one ever took the elevators except to haul boxes or bodies. Security cameras followed him step by step. Some were fixed view, studying doors, windows, and air conditioning grates. Others were controlled by humans. As he walked he could hear, or at least imagined he heard, the small motors moving the cameras.

He passed a few doors and gave a brief smile to a clerk carrying a handful of manila folders. His office was the third door past the corner where the bathrooms were. No doors were marked. If you looked at doors to find out where you were going, chances are you would be shot dead as an intruder. It paid to know what you were doing. He used the palm pad to gain access to his office.

As he entered, the lights came on to his personal standard. The internal sensors began adjusting the temperature to his liking, which was about four degrees cooler than what most people liked, even well-clad ones. Active brains, like high-end computers, require additional cooling. He sat at the desk, which was made to his personal criteria. It was a slab of steel three-quarters of an inch thick with rounded corners. It sat on two thirty-six-inch-diameter heavy wall steel pipes that had drawers custom fit into them. If the building collapsed around him, he would be well protected from an avalanche of debris in his personal refuge under the slab. The heavy steel could also stop any handgun round invented, should any attacker make it that far into the building.

He waved his hand towards the right-hand wall and instantly it transformed into a computer screen. The lights dimmed accordingly to enhance the image. With his index finger, he touched a spot on the steel surface of the desk. Faintly, the music of 10,000 Maniacs began playing from hidden speakers. Beneath the desk was a USB port into which he inserted the flash drive. His fingers flipped the business card around. As he read the numbers aloud, each one appeared in a grid on the wall screen. The screen fluttered for a brief moment and a dollar sign symbol appeared. A feminine voice spoke slightly louder than the music: "Money transferred."

While he had no doubts about that fact, it was always good to check. It was an odd part of the gray government business; if the money was not there, or got pulled by the supplier, there was very little recourse for a secret organization to sue for damages in a public arena. A single phone call would be made to seek rectification of the issue. If that failed, then blood would spill.

After scanning the flash drive for viruses or other issues, the computer opened a document that displayed on the wall screen. It was a table of contents. The gray-haired man placed the business card in his upper desk drawer and smiled. His protégé had learned well. He selected the first item listed and began to read. Hours later he sat back in his chair. It reclined a little. He waved his hand and the wall screen faded away. The other wall began to brighten with several primary colors that ebbed and flowed like liquid across the wall. Sensors in the headrest began reading certain brain waves, and the swirling lights began to dance and weave in time to them. Slowly, the lights changed their patterns and speed. His breathing and pulse slowed. After a few moments, he entered REM sleep. The computer continued to process the data on the flash drive in response to his programming.

Four hours passed. Washington, D.C., was now mostly asleep. Traffic noise rarely penetrated to this level in the building anyway, but at this hour few vehicles were passing by. Slowly the tempo of the lights increased, and even through his closed eyes his brain responded to the input. His brain waves increased and his pulse quickened slightly. In moments he was awake and fully rested.

An icon dimly flashed on the computer wall. He pointed at it and a file opened. "Correlate currently unassigned staff with mission requirements," he said aloud. The screen faded away and then pixels coalesced into a picture. It was Neah Bey. The gray-haired man placed his face into his hands, and then stared back at the screen. He spoke softly. "Select and advise." Then even more quietly, he added, "Sorry, my old friend."

————————

Omak adjusted the brightness of the monitor. The computer was unique, one of a kind, singular in its lack of identity. It looked like it came from Europe. There were no fancy labels of fruit or corporate logos; there were no model numbers, or references to gigabytes, RAM, CDs, DVRs, or any of the eye candy data that attracts buyers. It didn't even have a serial number. The inner workings were unmarked and handcrafted, made of standard parts available anywhere. In a sense, it did not exist. In a sense, neither did Omak.

He laid the envelope very carefully on the corner of the card table and stared at the computer. Omak sat on a five-gallon plastic bucket with a thick wad of newspapers to cushion his rump. From far away, his controller noticed him waiting. Even though the computer appeared to be off, it never really was. His controller turned on the monitor and typed in, "Nothing today. Nothing tomorrow. Maybe the day after." Then the monitor went blank. Omak knew he was still being watched, though the computer looked off.

———————

Omak was the son of a Chicago street cop. His mother had died at an early age, and he had needed to adapt to a father who was in the house, and then gone, and then back again on a very unpredictable schedule. He loved to hear from his father the stories of being a street crime-fighter, about fistfights, gunfights, sirens, handcuffs, and nightsticks. Sometimes his father brought him to the police range in the basement of the precinct station to fire a variety of guns. Omak became proficient with firearms in his youth. He dreamt of being a cop, too.

Omak read every crime novel and watched every cop show on television, and even used the internet to watch vintage black-and-white police shows like *Highway Patrol* with Broderick Crawford and every episode of *Dragnet* ever taped. Omak studied hard, and understood from his father that science and technology were going to be the keys to crime-fighting in the future. He became intrigued with biology, chemistry, and computer science while in junior high. Omak was a gifted athlete, greyhound-slim and strong. These attributes, combined with his tall, dark-haired good looks, made him the target of love-struck attention from countless girls in his high school class. However, he had his eyes and his heart set on just two things: becoming a Chicago cop like his dad, and marrying the girl across the hall in apartment 714.

———————

Roslyn was fair-skinned, thin, and pretty, and had a smile that would have been the pride of any orthodontist had she needed one. She too had plans, one of which was to follow her father in real estate and another of which was to marry the handsome young man across the hall in apartment 715.

Omak was accepted into the Chicago Police Academy and graduated with honors. As a rookie, he did not want to be the best, or rack up impressive arrest stats, or shoot people. He wanted to learn. When an opening came up for something outside his experience, he applied for it. When an assignment was not filled, he volunteered for it. He kept his physical skills sharp and worked out with a passion, and he took night classes, weekend classes, and online classes—anything he could do to learn. He eventually got his masters in police administration and was set to take the lieutenant's test when his father at dinner one evening complained of a pain in his left arm. In minutes, his father sagged out of his chair, dead from a massive coronary. The paramedics arrived and could do nothing.

The funeral was well attended by members of the Chicago Police Department, including chiefs, deputy chiefs, and most of the ranking officers. The saddest part for Omak was the terrible brevity of the condensed summary of his father's thirty years of service to the citizens of Chicago. It was a mere ten-minute ceremony. As he walked away from the gravesite, Roslyn came alongside him and held his hand.

"We, we should get married," Omak stammered.

"Okay," Roslyn replied. And that was that.

With one eye on the slope above him, he probed the snow to find the monocular. To his relief, he spotted the eerie demon eye glowing in the snow. Bey cleaned the lenses and looked at the nearest body. No movement. He waited. The pain pill began working its magic; he felt an odd calmness and warmth slowly replace the white-hot burn in his chest. Bey crawled slowly over to the body, and rolled it face up. He wiped the snow from the face and eyes. Out of respect for an adversary, a human working for his government just like Bey, he closed the eyes of the deceased. He found a small radio and an un-identified key.

The next body was face down like the first. Bey rolled it over and scowled. It was a young woman, maybe twenty to twenty-five years of age, pretty by Korean standards. He did a quick search and found a small kit bag attached to her belt. There were papers inside. Bey turned the mon-ocular over and used the green glow to light up the top page. It was his picture.

Later they would laugh about the timing and the com-plete lack of the honored dating rituals, the bended knee, and the engagement ring. It did, however, just seem right.

Omak had to settle the affairs of his father's estate. Sev-eral weeks after the funeral, there was a knock on the door, and to his surprise there was Roslyn with a suitcase and some paper bags tucked under her arms. Across the hall, Roslyn's mother smiled and waved. "Congratulations!" she said. Omak was a little taken aback. Roslyn pushed him out of the way and marched in with her few possessions.

She placed the suitcase on the floor and dropped the paper bags on the couch. Omak waved back to his not-quite-yet mother-in-law; "Thanks!" He closed the door and turned to face Roslyn with a few dozen questions on his mind. Those questions could wait until later. Roslyn had removed her summer dress and stood naked before him. The afternoon sun filtered through the curtains, dappling her skin in a shifting pattern of rose and amber. Roslyn opened her arms to him, and Omak moved into them without thinking. She whispered in his ear, "Promise that you will love me forever."

"I will." He kissed her neck. "I do." He kissed her again. "I intend to."

There weren't any pressing family traditions to contend with, so they saved a lot of money by having a simple wedding presided over by one of the department's chaplains. Roslyn's mom and dad took it all in stride, and never once suggested that the young couple adhere to a church wedding with all the frills and fanfare.

They stayed in his father's apartment. The landlord had liked the old man and rented many units to nice folk; he discouraged renters of questionable background by saying, "Yes, we have a number of Chicago's police officers as tenants." The landlord liked it when Omak walked through the lobby in uniform, and liked it even more when Omak invited his fellow cop friends to early morning coffee in the building's first floor espresso bar. A half dozen uniformed police officers in the espresso bar was very good for business.

Omak had to wait a year to get back on the list for the lieutenant's test, but it was not a wasted year. If he and Roslyn had been in love before, that love was a mere shadow of what had developed. Roslyn adorned the apartment with pictures of them and the places they went. Summer drives along the lake, their honeymoon at a Couples Resort in Jamaica, snowball fights, a few Chicago Bear's games; the photographs and mementos began covering the aging wallpaper.

Roslyn's career was taking hold, and she was promoted to a regional property management position with a large Midwest real estate firm. She did have to travel, which made for some lonely weekends. It did not matter to them; they made up for those times apart with spontaneous "dates" on the days they were together.

They had made an agreement to not start their family until after Omak made lieutenant. There were many long nights filled with studying, online courses, and intensive pre-testing given by fellow officers. In spite of the fact that the officers ultimately were competing against each other for promotions, the team player mentality always kicked in, and they helped each other. Finally the test dates arrived, and Omak did what his father had suggested he do: he partied like hell the weekend before, recovered, apologized to those he might have offended, and checked into a hotel by himself for one last run through the books. Good advice or not, it worked; Omak passed the test.

That was the first hurdle; each candidate was then interviewed, analyzed, and forced to wait until the promotion list appeared. When the list came out, Omak was number 75. This meant the department needed to have seventy-five open slots for lieutenants, and the funds to actually pay for the positions, in order for Omak to get promoted. Like all departments, the Chicago PD had a relationship with the bean counters at city hall that was sometimes good, and sometimes not. This was one of the times that rancor existed between the politicos at city hall and the department. Everyone was on pins and needles.

A measure of tragedy struck in Miami, Pittsburgh, and San Diego. Over the course of a month nearly seventy-five people were killed in street crimes in those cities. One major convention of architects and engineers that had been headed to San Diego decided that they should rethink those plans. A local candidate stood up at a campaign rally and said, "If we don't keep the Chicago Police Department strong, we will lose tourism and convention business to those towns that know how to fight crime!" Although a few short weeks later that particular candidate lost by a huge margin, the message had been sent. "Good Police Department equals Conventions at McCormick Place," not to mention full hotels, full bars, and well-paid hookers for all. Funding was added to the budget, and Omak was sworn in as a lieutenant. Magically, the ceremony took place twenty-five years after his father had achieved the same rank, almost to the day.

Roslyn beamed at the ceremony; Omak was given his new badge by a dear friend of his father, the deputy chief of the department. "Well, you are a little slower at getting the rank than your old man, but I can tell you are cut from the same cloth. Congratulations, Lieutenant Omak!" he said. Omak and a few fellow officers had dinner later at a pizza restaurant over towards Lake Michigan that for some reason had become the traditional spot for lieutenants to celebrate their promotions. The pizza was terrible, and the neighborhood was slightly better than a demilitarized zone in some third world country. Nevertheless, it was still a tradition. The cops lied about the taste of the pizza, they lied about how cold the beer was, and they lied about how well deserved some of the promotions were. Several of the wives and girlfriends had wisely rented a limo to cart their drunken boyfriends and husbands back home. Omak made it all the way to the door of the apartment before realizing that he was drunk out of his mind, could barely stand, and had to lean heavily against the door.

After he fumbled with his keys for several minutes, Roslyn opened the door. Without the support, Omak fell face first onto the floor of the apartment. He rolled sunny-side up and smiled. "I'm way drunk." Roslyn hauled his legs out of the doorway so she could close it. She grabbed a small pillow and lay down beside him. She lifted his head with one hand and slipped the pillow under with the other.

As Omak began slowly drifting away she said, "I'm pregnant."

He began to smile, and mouthed the words, "I'm gonna be a daddy."

While sitting in his office, Neah Bey noticed a flashing icon, indicating that a message waited for him on his computer. Attached to the side of the computer was a small thumb pad. The message only came through with the verification of his thumbprint. It would be unwise to cut off Bey's thumb and press it on the thumb pad in an effort to read his messages and take his calls. The office sat on top of a tank of natural gas that would level it as soon as the state of the thumb was detected. And it would look like an accident. With an extra thumb.

The Will of the United States is to work in, around, and through all the things that support the continuation of the United States. Now, Bey was given an assignment to work with any and all available resources to "investigate methods and achieve results in reducing burgeoning populations in outlined areas."

Attached to the message was a series of files to read that would self-delete in a time frame noted in the subject line. Usually there are a series of milestones attached to specific dates for the completion of an assigned task. In this message, there were none. Bey sat back. To achieve the desired final results of this task would take more years than he had left to live. But in those years there would be measurable and quantifiable results. The Will of the United States of America outlives its operatives.

He was given a list of books to read that would give him at least a cursory background on the subject. As was the custom for his operations, he ordered the books through Amazon.com and had them delivered to a rented post office box forty miles away. They arrived, and Bey began to read.

Bey discovered that populations can be described in five categories:

    1. Fast increasing

2. Increasing
3. Stable with swings
4. Declining
5. Disappearing

Bey was instructed to not consider categories 3, 4, and 5. Part of his study packet included a map of the world; there were a number of areas that were marked 1 and 2. Some were in the Western Hemisphere, and some were not. In the part of the brief that generally encapsulated the Will of the United States, Neah Bey was directed to simply "mitigate."

At first glance, it appeared to be a rather daunting task for an individual. But they don't employ people like Bey to be faint of heart; they employ people who have the ability to perform. And miracles were the rule rather than the exception.

––––––––––

Palix Van Trump was born into an Amish family in Lancaster County, Pennsylvania. The family was open to the outside world and did not fully embrace the strict doctrines that prohibited the use of electricity, diesel-powered farm equipment, and automobiles. This attitude somewhat distanced them from their Amish neighbors. On the other hand, many of the Amish girls were very comfortable riding with Palix in his family's car to go out for ice cream and the occasional movie behind their parents' backs. Palix saw the harshness of the Amish lifestyle and felt that it was not for him; he wanted a little more latitude to perform, and a little larger arena to play in. Instead of following the local tradition of dropping out of school in the eighth grade, he continued on through high school.

His grades were good enough for him to get a scholarship to Penn State. There, his studies centered on what he knew best: faith and the Bible. As graduation approached, a lot of his college friends were scrambling for jobs, trying to figure out where to get the best salary package—the one with the greatest perks, the best retirement deal, the best parking spot, and more. His faith was the preeminent driving force in his life, but Palix Van Trump was very deeply steeped in the Amish traditions of practicality, which helped him decide to enter the monastery; one had to pick the path of least resistance and go for the long haul. Ensconced within the walls and the embrace of the church, he began a life of comfort without too much strife, without too much worry about layoffs, and with a modest but consistent salary and benefits. And he could park wherever he wanted with his special state clergy license plates.

At times he traveled home and visited his family and friends, and there he was sometimes ostracized for apparently being a traitor to his faith. It did not matter; he had some money in the bank and three squares a day. Life was fairly calm, and there were few bumps in the road. His excellent reading and writing skills made his efforts to write sermons for himself and others easy. He was often called upon to write sermons not only for his own church, but for surrounding churches as well. Sometimes late at night his phone would ring and there would be an urgent request for him to travel either near or far to fill in when a priest took ill or was called away for some emergent condition. Palix set up emergency outlets during disasters like Hurricane Katrina and the Haitian earthquake. He worked hard at what he did, and was recognized for it with periodic elevations in position unusual for such a young man.

Palix Van Trump had a character flaw; he did not just accept the trials and tribulations of the priesthood at face value. He wanted more. He was sent to a church in New York City, near Times Square and the Theater District. There he wrote and delivered sermons and conducted Bible studies for a grand array of humanity. Artists, dancers, actors, corporate heads, art gallery owners, producers, directors, designers, people of wealth and stature—all were members of the various congregations for the benefit of whom Palix plied his craft. New York City was a long way from Lancaster County, Pennsylvania.

Sometimes he was called upon to organize informal backstage meetings of performers at various theaters. These were just ten-minute services for those in traveling troupes. It was exciting to be backstage amid the sets and costumes. Stagehands sweated and pulled and tugged at heavy weights used to counterbalance props, makeup artists scurried after performers, and some people, scarcely visible under mounds of gaudy dresses and animal costumes, wound their way around the melee behind the purple drapes.

Palix volunteered for such duties as time permitted; he enjoyed seeing all the glamour and occasionally rubbing elbows with real stage stars. However, such glamour could become addictive, such attention could foster profoundly unhealthy appetites, and such was the case for Palix Van Trump.

A few members of a cast were leaving to rejoin the major part of the troupe in Florida, and their travel plans precluded attending normal services at the church. A handwritten phone number that went directly to Palix's cell phone was pinned up in a dressing room for use in just such instances. Palix set down his microwave dinner and installed his white clerical collar and was out the door in five minutes. He sometimes followed the local theater scene from his laptop or picked up information as he walked from one appointment to another in the area. He would not have shied away from any call for duty. Sometimes the nature of the show dictated that he slip in through the back door or conceal his calling under a billowing trench coat. It would lack a measure of propriety if the local priest were seen entering a theater where drugs, alcohol, or nudity was the main theme of the performance. In this case, Palix was unaware of the nature of the play, but chose to be safe and turn up the collar of his coat before nodding to the security guard at the door, who opened it for him. The main floor had given way from the audience to maintenance personnel who were sweeping the floors, picking up programs left in the seats, and readying the theater for the next performance.

He slipped between the curtains to the right of the stage and climbed up the seven lucky steps to the main stage. Roadies were moving large wheeled crates around, taking down light supports, and handling smaller loads with hand dollies. Behind the rear screen were a collection of folding chairs and crates loaded and empty that would serve as the sanctuary for this evening's service. A couple of heavily tattooed roadies were already seated. One of the musicians leaned on a crate, and three female performers sat in the chairs. Palix smiled as he walked up to the makeshift podium, which consisted of a large wheeled shipping container topped with a milk crate that was propped up with a pair of shoes to give it an angle. Other more conservative members of the clergy would have walked out, claiming that the lack of formality was not conducive to a proper service. This was an area where Palix excelled, it was his turf, off the cuff: craft the message to the listener, and accept the environment for what it was—simply a church in a different disguise.

Palix looked over the small congregation and noted the roadies, sweaty and smelling of cigarettes and pot. The musician looked on the verge of some sort of caffeine-induced psychosis, with a Rock Star in each hand. The seated girls were young, lithe, and graceful. The young woman in the center was Asian, and very pretty. Adhering to his typical introduction, he asked that each person introduce himself or herself by giving just his or her name and hometown. He only half listened as his attention was drawn to the pretty Asian woman.

Her name was Yin Lao; she was the daughter of Vietnamese refugees, and she was beautiful. It was clear that she wore nothing under the thin robe that slid barely halfway down her thighs. She had strong-looking legs, like most dancers. Palix began his brief sermon. His gaze often traveled up and down the smooth legs of Yin Lao. Possibly she was just teasing the young priest, possibly not; nevertheless she leaned forward, allowing the robe to fall to expose the delicate curve of her breasts. Palix tried to avert his eyes, but like the proverbial moth facing the flame he could not shake the allure of such beauty.

The sermon ended on its usual high note of hope. Palix smiled and thanked everyone. He closed his Bible, braced against the milk crate, and tried to gently wipe the perspiration from his forehead with his coat sleeve. The musician and two of the roadies shook his hand, thanking him for coming out late at night and providing them with a brief sermon. Palix looked around and did not see where Yin Lao had gone. Somewhat deflated, he tidied up his notes and wrapped himself in his coat and headed out the side door of the theater.

He decided to take a cab, and as he raised an arm to flag one down he felt a tug on his sleeve. Yin Lao had managed to dress in skintight black pants and a soft pink sweater that had a plunging neckline. A large single pearl hung on a gold chain between her breasts.

"Yes? I mean, excuse me, can I help you?" He reddened in the face, embarrassed by his stammering.

Yin Lao laced her arm in his. "Can we talk a little more? How about coffee or tea?" she asked. She nodded towards an all-night espresso-deli next to the theater entrance.

"Well, I'm not sure, it is late and I have other duties." His voice trailed off. Smitten as he was, Palix Van Trump was already past the point of rescue or redemption. Within the hour they were sweating, naked in her apartment, loosely wrapped in soft cotton sheets. And so began Palix Van Trump's slide, as Yin Lao had appetites beyond his wildest dreams, appetites that the salary of a young priest could ill afford.

They came to him one afternoon, armed with nothing more than a thick folder of receipts and some photographs. The three men made it very clear that Palix Van

Trump was going to go with them to the Vatican, or Palix Van Trump was going to jail for a very long time. He was not told what he was going to be doing at the Vatican, but it most certainly had to be better than a jail sentence. Palix regretted later, as did his fellow fallen teammates, that he had not chosen jail time over interminable servitude to the old man. He never heard of or saw Yin Lao again, but then his access to movies, television, and theater publications was at best limited.

As they escorted him away, the eldest of the three motioned them all to stop, and with a flick of the wrist removed Palix's white collar tab. "You no longer are a priest. Consider yourself lucky."

Twenty-four hours later, Palix was shown his small cloister and how to follow the hallways to his new office. It reeked of smoke. When he traced his fingers across his desk, black soot stuck to his fingertips. His escort leaned forward and whispered, "benvenuti all inferno." *Welcome to Hell.*

───────────

Neah sipped his coffee and read the brief again. "Hmm, rather an interesting proposition." Although once an agent received a task it wasn't really a proposition, it was a directive. The importance of the mission was clear: various friendly and unfriendly countries' populations were going to pose a threat to the United States. "Yes," Neah smiled, "even our friends can be threats." In this case, the threat was non-military. In order to preserve resources, namely air, water, oil, and land, methods would have to be created to modify population growth patterns.

For various reasons—economic, social, and religious—

people just could not figure this out themselves. It was up to Bey, and the Will of the United States of America, to fix the problem.

The nearest problem area was in South America, and in parts of those lands to the south of the Rio Grande River. Bey flew to Rio, wandered around the slums, sat in on a few church services, and studied in the library. The combination of abject poverty and fundamentalist religious views was a dangerous mixture. In order to advance the religious beliefs, and fund future growth, more people were needed in the Church. More people in the Church meant less for everyone else to eat and drink safely. An unfortunate spiral resulted wherein impoverished areas berift of useful resources became overpopulated. The Church condemned birth control of any sort as a violation of creed. On the other hand, having an entire population starve appeared to be okay.

Bey never understood this balancing of the scales of quality and quantity of life by the narrow-minded and ensconced powerful. Clearly they believed that millions of uninformed starving people were a far better result than a moderately well-fed and educated population. "Ah, there's the rub." Neah perched his readers on the middle of his nose. "Education, the root of all evil."

Everything went as could be expected with the pregnancy, the doctor's visits, the emotional highs and lows, the fussing with baby clothes, the baby showers, and the baby room things. Omak was initially a little concerned about Roslyn's parents living right across the hall, but never once did they barge in, stop by unexpectedly, or stay too late. Indeed, they had to be asked to come over.

When Omak got used to the idea of having a family, Roslyn's father sent him an email inviting him down to the espresso bar for a cup of coffee on Saturday morning. "He could have just knocked on the door, couldn't he?" asked Omak. Roslyn looked over his shoulder and read the email.

"Well, he is just being polite. Maybe he heard us last night." She bit his ear and darted away. Omak turned crimson, the flush starting at his neck and moving up the sides of his face.

"Oh, yeah, last night!" He leered at Roslyn. "Want to see if the police are called here tonight?"

Omak liked Roslyn's father, Kelso; he was witty, and very intelligent. Kelso was already seated at a small table near the large window that looked out over the street. During the spring and fall the windows could be rolled back and patrons could reach out and shake the hands of friends passing by. Kelso waved Omak over; as was their custom they shook hands, and then Omak sat down. Kelso clasped his hands and leaned his chin against his knuckles. "Wow, a grandchild! How terrifying!" He rolled his eyes heavenward and laughed. "We were just about your age when we had Roslyn. That was a time. Ethel out of work, looking like she had shoplifted a watermelon, hell, two watermelons!" His eyes darted around the espresso bar. "For God's sake don't tell her I said that, she still gets flaming mad when I mention it!" They laughed. Kelso continued to chat. "I had just started with the firm, nose to the grindstone, shoulder to the wheel, eye on the prize, not knowing what was important, and what wasn't. Dead broke and madly in love."

He grew a little quieter. "Those were the most fun days of our lives, having Roslyn, juggling her into and out of the top drawer of the dresser, which was her crib. Oh, we were horrible parents, we let her crawl on the floor, smacked her butt when she was bad, denied her watching the television, all the stuff you go to jail for now, I suppose."

Omak laughed. "As a matter of fact, it's a capital crime in South Carolina to deny your child a widescreen TV!" It was Kelso's turn to laugh.

"Well," Kelso began, "Ethel and me kind of figured that you two kids were meant for each other. Oh, it wasn't like we were spying on you. You just made it so obvious. If Roslyn ever left the apartment, you would open your door a smidge and watch her go down the hall. And to tell the truth, she watched you too!" They laughed together and sipped their drinks. "Ethel was worrying that you two would never figure out your feelings for each other. At one time she even asked if there was something wrong with both of you!" Kelso saw a friend walk by the window, and he exchanged waves with the other man and his wife. "So, let's cut to the chase." Kelso fumbled in his shirt pocket and brought out a check and a business card. "I'm not much for all this small talk, so here is a check that will cover our granddaughter Lacey's college education. I have attached a business card from an old friend who says if you and he manage the money it may even pay for a master's degree, if you are careful. "

Omak stammered, "Uh? Lacey? We are having a girl? We are having a girl named Lacey?"

Kelso looked at Omak with a dead serious look on his face and then broke into a belly laugh. "How the hell should I know? I'm just jerking you around!"

Omak smiled and said, "Good one, Kelso, good one." The check, however, was real.

When the little girl-child arrived, Ethel and Kelso came to the hospital to pay a visit. When they entered the birthing suite, Roslyn stopped nursing and handed the child to her mother. "Mom and Dad, meet Lacey. Del picked out the name himself." Kelso turned ash gray.

Ethel said, "What a lovely name for such a pretty young girl! How did you ever come up with it?"

Del smiled and said, "Oh, a good cop has many sources for such things." He elbowed Kelso in the ribs.

———

In five years, Omak made captain and took over a special victims unit. This severely impacted his family time, so he, Roslyn, and Lacey made the most of their time together. While religion itself was not an issue, Ethel and Kelso wanted Lacey to at least attend the neighborhood church and make an informed decision about her religious beliefs herself. Omak and Roslyn agreed, and generally the duty fell to Roslyn to take Lacey to church.

———

Bey toured the eastern Amazon basin and then up into Central America. A common religion misled and oppressed native, Spanish, and Portuguese populations. Even though Bey was nondescript in his appearance, he could not hide his research, the books he read, or the places he visited. And the Church had more operatives than the entire population of the United States.

He flew out of Central America and back down to Colombia, then over to Brasilia. He had never been far upriver in the Amazon basin from the Atlantic Ocean side, so Bey charted a small floatplane and headed up the river for a three or four day trip. This was what he called "the investigation of the root cause." Here, remote from the rest of the world, with little TV, scarce internet, and limited outside contact, he would find the baseline issue.

The message was sent through the heavens, something the Sister thought privately amusing, to the South American administrative arm of the Church. There, it was attached to other messages from all the other churches, bundled into an electronic package, and sent off to Italy. There it was copied, filed, archived, and forwarded to dozens upon dozens of planners, schedulers, schemers and dreamers of the sort that make up the administrative side of any huge conglomerate.

One copy of this particular amassed report covering thousands of smaller reports from around the globe came to the computer of the old man. Over the years he had received tens of thousands, maybe hundreds of thousands, of such reports. Yet, in this chaff of information he sometimes found something useful.

He thought back into his considerable memory and recalled reading other such messages from this very

Sister, and their chance meeting, how many decades ago? In quiet moments, he had read about the flowers, the birds, and the recent painting of the church in that small and distant village east of the Andes. His eyes rapidly scanned the monitor and just as rapidly discarded the numbers and names. Abruptly he stopped. The steel gray eyes backtracked up the page. He pulled the words together into a form in his mind: Americans, new well, fewer orphans.

He smirked at the comment the Sister had made about the efforts of the priest to promote fidelity amongst the locals. If there was anything he had come to know over the years, it was that no amount of Bible thumping and caterwauling from a priest in an impoverished village at the edge of society was going to impact the people's decadent desire to attempt to procreate as often as possible. His few good fingers strummed the desktop.

In moments, he typed out an inquiry for the programmers to work on. He flagged the file "MEO" which stood for "My Eyes Only," the most secret level of internal communications. As always, he used the superior resources of the American computer system to run the query than that of the Vatican. The programmers who would handle these files in that system had no interest in them whatsoever. The old man typically relied on outsourcing his research to other parts of the Church.

Here in Vatican City, everyone had an agenda to become closer to the pope. The old man brought up a map of the world on his overly large monitor, and within seconds dots appeared where the Church had orphanages of any size. He sat back on the simple wooden chair and stared at the screen. Data streamed past him on his monitor. Dots on the screen began to change color. The old man's brow furrowed deeply.

———————

The pilot was too curious. He talked a lot about this and that, and every now and then inserted a specific question on who Bey was, where he was from, and what he was doing. "You, sir, read a lot of books on people," he observed.

They set down in the river and drifted over to the decrepit collection of odd-sized lumber that served this backwater as a dock. From there Neah Bey walked into the village. A tavern, a store, but no school, though there was a church, much in need of paint and a new roof. The Church tried to hold some classes, heavily tilted towards religious dogma and offering little if anything else. The children were already being ground into the soil: slash, burn, starve, and pray. Bey smiled at an elderly woman wearing a worn habit as she tended to the flowers along the edge of the road.

———————

The monsignor and the young priest ventured out the next morning to recover the body of the mayor. During the night, the younger man had cried as he tried to wash the blood splatters from his vestments. The mayor was a Church member, and had been most generous even when times were difficult. They dragged the body into the sanctuary, pausing only to watch the commandant drive by. This time he did not tip his hat. Several townspeople took buckets of water into the town square and flushed the blood away.

In the following month, the Germans acquired several

of the larger homes and those apartments over the stores on the town square to house the officers and higher-ranking enlisted men. The school was turned into an armory, and classes were held in the church as space permitted. Food rations were cut in half, and then in half again. Several times, many of the men, women, and children who crowded the church left with empty bowls. Winter descended from the high mountains and gave the area its first blanket of snow of the year.

Letters arrived occasionally from other churches describing better or worse conditions. The monsignor took the young priest into private council and told him there were rumors of terrible things happening to the Jews in other areas. They would have to act soon or the weather would make travel nearly impossible. The monsignor was not elderly but was certainly too far past his prime to be traveling anywhere during inclement weather. Nonetheless, the monsignor planned to take a group of parents and children over the low pass and then have them make their way southward towards the border between France and Italy. From there, they would travel as best they could further south, using local churches as waypoints. It was a precarious situation; the local Germans had not made any overt threats against anyone, other than the mayor. Indeed, although the rations were meager, there was enough stored food in the village to allow everyone there to at least survive the winter, but just barely. The young priest urged caution, but the monsignor was a devout and committed man. The monsignor wanted to save as many of his villagers as he could, church members or not.

———————

Bey played the tourist and wandered through the dismal market, which offered a small variety of fruits and vegetables along with some jungle meat of questionable origin and hygiene. Every step he took he was engulfed; a gaggle of begging children surrounded him. When they pressed too closely, Bey took a handful of the lowest denomination of the local coin and threw it in the opposite direction. The squabble diverted attention from him. This gave Bey a break from being tugged at and pawed over. He brought up a small camera and snapped some shots of the children, the church, and the market.

Bey eventually returned to the plane and put back his disposable camera while giving his bags a quick once-over. The pilot told Bey not to worry; he had watched the plane the whole time. Bey knew this was true. When Bey had climbed the steeple of the church, he had pulled out his monocular and watched the pilot go through his entire set of luggage.

For an unsophisticated backwater pilot, he used a very nice miniature digital camera on all the papers Bey had tucked away in his work case. Pity. Bey had long been schooled in carrying papers that were signed with magnificent flourishes and had official-looking seals. Most were items he had pulled from dumpsters behind dormitories at the University of Washington, in Seattle. However, to the uninformed, they looked very interesting.

They were spooled up and heading downriver into the slight breeze coming up the channel. The turboprop was in good shape; the plane was pretty much a standard single-engine hopper with floats. "So, what is it that brings you to the Amazon, senhor? You do not look or act like the tourist, no? You look in all the funny places for a long time and at the usual places for hardly any."

The plane took to the air, and they followed the river at a low altitude at Bey's request. "Sightseeing, you know?" Bey smiled broadly at the pilot and said, "Yes, that is true. I do look at things differently." Bey checked his GPS against the agency-supplied maps and satellite photos. He calculated that they were about halfway between villages of any size. From his chest pocket, Bey took out his favorite Bittner Namiki pen and clicked it open as if to make a note on the map. The pilot leaned over and stuck out a manicured nail and pointed to where they were going. It's not often that a bush pilot would have to get a manicure, much less find a place in a bush pilot's usual haunts to have one done.

Bey stabbed the back of the pilot's hand with the pen. He then dropped the pen and grabbed the control yoke. The pilot gasped, retracted his hand, and began to convulse. Pink foam dribbled from his nostrils and out of the corner of his mouth. He was dead in less than three minutes. Neurotoxins have that effect. Leaning over the pilot, Bey managed to unclip the pilot's seatbelt and open the door. He tipped the plane into a quick roll to the left, and the dead pilot fell out into the river from about fifty feet up. Bey jerked the plane back over to the right, and the open door slammed closed.

After a horrific night at work in which a deranged mother killed three of her children and severely wounded another, Omak was headed back to the neighborhood to pick up Roslyn and Lacey. They had plans to pick up some impromptu picnic ingredients so they could enjoy some family time at the lake while Lacey fed the birds. He parked across the street and waited for church to let out.

———————

Kent Shelton had lost his job, and with the little money he had left proceeded to get drunk and high at the same time. His girlfriend told him not to come around her place again unless he had a job, and certainly not while under the influence. Kent was in a drunken hophead rage when he stomped on the gas pedal of the old Ford and laid a patch of rubber all the way down the block in front of his former girlfriend's house. A Chicago motorcycle cop was on the next block over and heard the screaming tires and roaring engine. He gave chase. Shelton looked in his rear-view mirror and said, "Ah, fuck me." He then downshifted, and the pursuit was on. The motorcycle cop radioed the chase to the precinct, and five other police units began converging to cut Shelton off.

Shelton sideswiped some newspaper boxes, which shattered and sent a cascade of newsprint into the air. The motorcycle cop swerved expertly and began to crowd up on Shelton's bumper, siren wailing.

———————

Del had his police radio down low so he could hear the last refrains of the recessional and know when to start his car. He did not hear of the pursuit until sirens blocked out the church music. The church doors opened, and Roslyn and Lacey were the first out. Del opened the car door and held his hands up to keep his wife and daughter on the opposite curb. Lacey, in her youthful impatience, darted between parked cars and ran into the road. Roslyn stared into Del's eyes for the smallest portion of a second and then gave chase to her daughter. Shelton lost control of the car halfway down the block, and it slid sideways down the street. Del was struck by the front bumper and was thrown free. He was unconscious when his head hit the windshield of the second car he collided with. His wife and daughter were killed instantly.

———————

Shelton's car rolled a few times, and he was ejected from the wreckage. He escaped with only a few bumps and a handful of small lacerations. When the police surrounded him, he began vomiting. His last words before passing out were, "You see that? The goofy bitch threw her kid in front of my car!"

———————

Omak was in a coma for two weeks. The doctors spoke to the numerous visitors.

"Yes, we think he'll be fine."

"Yes, we are hoping for a full recovery."

And, "No, he does not feel any pain. We think he can hear you but he may not be able to understand."

The department chaplain who had married Roslyn and Del stopped by nearly every day and prayed. Officers, secretaries, even file clerks all passed through the private room where he lay. Some brought flowers, others cards. Ethel and Kelso stopped by more than the others. Del was their last link to their daughter and granddaughter. Sometimes when fellow officers spoke, they could see his eyes move beneath the taped-down lids. It wasn't clear whether this was because Del heard or partially heard what they were saying, but somehow it made them feel better about talking to their friend. On the thirteenth day, a captain leaned close over Del so that no one else could hear.

"Just so you know, old friend, we beat the fuck out of Shelton yesterday, and today, and we will do it again tomorrow."

Omak's hand closed tightly over his brother captain's. During the two weeks of his coma, in spite of medical professionals' opinions to the contrary, every second Omak's brain was filled with an endless loop of the last violent images of his wife and child being killed, over and over and over again. When he emerged, he was changed.

Back in Seattle, Bey read voraciously on the subject of population and population controls. This is what he was assigned to do, to become literate on the subject. He then read material that was focused on the religious elements of large families and the prohibitions against birth control. Even if you were starving, having children provided a path for you into heaven. In some cultures, your children were your retirement system. The more kids, the greater your ease in your not so golden years.

It always worked out better for the Church if the next generation was just as uneducated and malleable as the last. There had to be a wedge that would separate the current behavior from the better behavior of the future. The trick was to create a wedge that only Bey and the gray government knew about. Over time, there would be red flags, consternation, investigations, and more. It would be better to turn the direction of the masses without their knowledge. It was even better to have the masses buy into a portion of what you were trying to do, by lies and deceit if necessary.

Bey took his wife, Ione, to the coast for a three-day weekend, and to watch their niece play in a baseball tournament with her community college team. Neah liked to watch her play, and her selfless teamwork. Ione sat and chatted for hours with her sisters. As they usually did, the extended family went out to eat together after the game. The rest of the weekend was spent prowling antique stores and quilt shops. Neah had a fairly large collection of metalwork from the 1950s and 1960s. Syrup pitchers, lunchboxes, measuring cups, and gravy shakers adorned his part of the kitchen. Bey was always on the lookout for an ancient set of metal salt and pepper shakers.

Omak spent the better part of a month in the hospital's physical therapy department. He was stretched, iced, walked, cajoled, and intimidated by a variety of therapists, whose efforts were all aimed at returning the body to active duty. None of his bodily injuries were going to leave anything more than scars visible to the naked eye. But Omak's wounds went deeper than any physical therapist could reach. And scars from those wounds would never heal.

Kelso and Ethel and a few of Omak's fellow officers made a sort of pilgrimage with Omak from the hospital to his apartment. Omak was quite able to stand and move about with his cane. He shook hands, received pats on the back, and politely noted the flowers and cards that were set about the apartment. When the door was finally closed, Omak stood in the front room of a place that he no longer considered home. He looked about the room and methodically began turning all the pictures of his wife and child to the wall.

When that task was completed, he stood in the center of what was once his one and only world. Tears burned down his face like salt acid.

One of the better ploys to use in moving a population is to use its beliefs against it. Backed up by the Will of the United States, Neah and his associates had moved mountains.

Today, he sat outside and watched the neighbor lady, Joyce, hang up some clothes on her sunporch. Ione was grubbing around and torturing some small potted plant nearby. Ione noticed the neighbor lady, and she waved to her. Joyce waved back. Neah waved only because he enjoyed watching Joyce's breasts wiggle back and forth under her thin blouse. Neah Bey may have been a sinister agent of the gray arm of the government, but nice boobs were still nice boobs.

Joyce shouted, "You know, cleanliness is next to godliness!" Bey laughed and waved again. Joyce waved back again.

lone kicked his chair and said under her breath, "You pervert." Bey smiled.

The data appeared to be scant more than random collections of numbers smeared across the monitor. Still, the old man stared at it until his eyes watered. The evidence was clear, and even though it sat before him, it was impossible to believe. Forty-five percent of all orphanages within the sphere of the Church and its subsidiaries were showing declines in the number of children being admitted. He scrolled through the data for more than a day.

On his computer, he made small notations next to statements he planned to investigate. The old man pressed the button on his desk and summoned his young assistant. As always, the young man entered and never looked directly at him, always at some point over his head. He passed over a flash drive containing his queries and motioned the assistant away. He stared at the closed door for many moments and pondered what must happen next. His gaze returned to the monitor and slowly, laboriously, he began shaping the data into something cogent. The old man knew that raw data was somewhat suspect, and one could be drawn into a conclusion based on outliers in any set.

With a handful of keystrokes, he eliminated a series of entries that dealt with natural disasters, forced evacuations, rising rivers, churches closing and sending orphans to other facilities, and more. The data scrambled and reorganized itself. The old man startled for a moment and slammed his damaged hand down on the desk loudly. Clearly, God was not involved with this mischief. Using computational capabilities equal to those of some entire countries, he ordered correlations between the falling numbers and any charitable efforts conducted by anyone within a day's walk of the orphanages. The results stunned him. Someone was bringing an end to the Church by means as yet unclear. How could clean drinking water reduce a population's explosive growth? It made no sense at all.

It was three in the morning. Seattle weather being what it is meant that it was raining. One of the cats had curled up under his arm and was snoring like a drunken sailor. Bey was tossing and turning a little. Insomnia is a common trait of people with lots of responsibilities or guilty consciences.

Joyce had said, "Cleanliness is next to godliness." Neah remembered his mother telling him that when he was a child. Bey slipped from the bed as quietly as he could. On-line, he scheduled a flight to Washington, D.C.

A defense attorney was appointed for Shelton and convinced him to serve three years for a much lesser charge than the twenty five years the state prosecutors sought. The fact that the victims were the wife and child of a decorated Chicago police captain weighed little on the court administrators, who had to adjust schedules, find jurors, and battle mountains of paperwork. In the end, they were just glad to have one less case to handle.

Captain Omak read the sentencing sheet when it came up on his email. Without comment, he deleted it. He then made an appointment in his computer schedule for two years and eight months in the future. Omak then resumed his duties.

Omak used his official connections to make sure he knew exactly where Kent Shelton was, and where he was headed. He used his considerable influence to make sure Shelton's life was a living hell inside the walls.

Ethel and Kelso died within a few months of each other, leaving Omak with nothing and no one. Although he didn't need the money, he began selling off furnishings, pictures, and all the things that Roslyn and Lacey had brought to the apartment. He disposed of Ethel and Kelso's estate and began consolidating his wealth into a few bank accounts. He exercised a variety of contacts to get fictitious driver licenses, passports, and alternate identities. Omak had only a few desires: to seek revenge, and to disappear. At work he wore a mask of professionalism and carried himself as if nothing really had happened. This did not fool his fellow officers; they knew he was a changed man. They knew they were only seeing a fragment of what was really going on.

Omak changed assignments and began working directly with the medical examiners and pathologists who were assigned to investigate the natural and unnatural deaths of people. He studied and he learned.

While he was working on a "mundane" murder, wherein a drunk woman had knifed her drunk boyfriend, Omak's computer chirped. He clicked the icon to find that the two years and eight months had come and gone. Omak sat back, looked about his office. A fire began to burn inside him. What had been a small coal of anger grew into a conflagration until it consumed what was left of Delano "Del" Omak. He had four months to prepare for the release of Kent Shelton.

Omak waited in the alley near the fleabag hotel where Kent Shelton hung out. Behind him was an old Chevy van that had local license plates registered to a bakery ten blocks away. Street cops typically overlooked local plates and registrations. Omak checked his watch and knew from weeks of following Shelton that he would be staggering home soon from his favorite bar two blocks over. At least for the past two weeks it had been his favorite bar. Some unknown person had given him an unlimited tab there. Life was great for Kent Shelton, everybody loved him, and everywhere he turned, he had friends.

As Shelton passed an alley, he felt a sharp bite on his thigh. He winced and looked down to see a syringe stuck in his leg. "What the …" he exclaimed. He fell back into the alley. Strong hands grabbed him and pulled him further backwards into the darkness. Whatever drug he had been given made him limp. Through the drug and alcohol haze, he could see everything, hear everything, and feel everything. He would be begging in a few hours to be dead.

Omak stripped Shelton and put his clothes on. He would masquerade as Shelton long enough to clean out whatever personal effects Shelton had in his room. Omak did not worry about being stopped or questioned. On the streets, people tended to stick to their own business and not look too closely or care too much about the people around them. As far as the police department was concerned, Shelton was going to be a missing person that no one important was going to miss at all, one whom no one was going to spend a whole lot of time looking for. If he showed up dead, no one would shed tears.

Omak had rented a small industrial storage unit. Omak did not want to be disturbed. Shelton was strapped into a chair very reminiscent of an old-style wooden electric chair, which is what Omak had modeled it from. The drug prevented Shelton from speaking, begging, or screaming, but it would soon wear off, as would the liquor-induced haze.

Omak waited until Kent Shelton was fully conscious, fully awake, and fully capable of seeing, hearing, and *feeling*. With masterful precision, Omak forced open Shelton's jaw and tore his vocal cords out of his throat. All Shelton could do was make wheezing noises that created a faint vapor of blood. Omak left the torn flesh on Shelton's bare arm. An intravenous drip paralyzed Shelton but left him still able to feel everything. Shelton's entire body was frozen and incapable of movement, except for his eyes, which followed Omak's every move as he headed towards the door. Frozen, unable to move, but not numb. The rough wood chafed his buttocks, the rope bit deeply into his arms and ankles.

Omak smiled at his victim and then turned a couple of timers on a panel near the door. Omak left. In the darkness adjacent to the door was a barely discernible cloth drape covering something. Shrill squeaks, rustling, and scurrying noises emanated from under the covering. A timer clicked, and bright light pierced the gloom and cast a beam, illuminating the room and the cloth covering. Another timer made a loud click, and the covering lifted away. The covering had kept from view a large plastic dog kennel customized so that one entire side was fitted with clear acrylic. Inside the kennel were a dozen large ghetto rats gnawing at their prison, gnawing on each other. The beam blinded Shelton a little. Off to his side, a mirror slowly turned towards him, but not so he could see his face. Shelton looked into the mirror and was confused for a moment; his genitals had been smeared with peanut butter. Another click and the door of the cage opened, and then the lights went out. From the van, Omak looked at his watch and waited until he could just discern the last sounds Kent Shelton would ever make.

Omak returned a few days later and was not really surprised to see some very well fed rats, and a very dead Kent Shelton. Omak left the door open and turned on all the lights. In a few minutes, the rats found their way back into the alleyway and their dumpster environment. Omak unbuckled the mutilated corpse of Shelton and folded him neatly into the multiple layers of plastic he had previously stretched across the floor. Wisely, he had placed several inches of kitty litter around Shelton in order to soak up whatever dripped off.

In minutes, he had loaded Shelton into the van, disassembled the chair into a dozen different odd pieces, and folded up the kennel as flat as it would go. With all the physical evidence tucked away, Omak put on a face respirator and pulled a high-pressure hose out of the van. He sprayed the ceiling, beams, light fixtures, walls, floors, door, and walkway of the storage unit with commercial-strength bleach. At two in the morning, in an industrial area known for being a high crime area, no one of merit was going to complain.

Three hours later, in a fictitiously rented boat, Omak was out on the lake where the water was very deep. Shelton had been tied into a sandwich of chain link fencing. Omak struggled with getting Shelton's remains over the side and tied it off with a single quick release hook. Heavy chains with concrete blocks were affixed to every corner of the chain link sandwich and stretched across the middle of it in an "X" pattern. Without ceremony, other than staring directly into Kent Shelton's lifeless eyes, Omak released the body and anchor and watched it fade quickly into the watery gloom. With a thin smile, Omak watched as Shelton wafted and sank towards the mush at the bottom of Lake Michigan, six hundred and six feet down.

Back in the city, Omak drove down a dozen alleys, placing single pieces of the chair and crate into different alleyway dumpsters. The kitty litter he took to the back of a butcher shop. He tore open the wrappers that held the contaminated kitty litter and poured it into a dumpster that contained approximately eight hundred pounds of butcher shop floor sweepings. As soon as Omak pulled out of one end of an alley, a garbage truck pulled in the other. Within hours, all the remains of Omak's work had been processed, sorted, and containerized and were heading to different landfills scattered across the Midwest.

Omak resigned from the Chicago Police Department eight months later. He hung around long enough to make sure that no bright and upcoming police cadet was going to stumble upon his illicit activities. Two months after Kent

Shelton disappeared, a report was generated that said he was missing. Since Shelton's rent had not been paid, the landlady opened the room and, seeing nothing of value, rented it on the spot to a crackhead and his girlfriend. A report was filed that suggested Shelton might have moved out of the area, possibly to someplace near the water. Omak was inwardly pleased with his wry joke. At this point, the deep lake critters had long since disposed of anything other than bones, which would remain in the deep muck of the lake bottom forever.

Omak was now free of the world. He had his money and his multiple identities, and he was angry. He wanted someone, anyone, to pay for what had happened to him and his family. He raged inside against the prosecutors for the plea bargain that shortened the suffering of Kent Shelton. He cursed the EMTs, the paramedics, the nurses, and all the doctors that failed to save his pretty wife and young daughter. He despised his own brothers in the police department for failing to stop Kent sooner. Hollowed out by hatred, he sought a release. He was just lacking a *belonging*.

He made a fast trip around Chicago and was gone, off the grid. Before leaving, he stopped by the church where the closed-casket funerals of Roslyn and Lacey had been held. The road had been repaved, new awnings for different businesses had sprouted up, and still the neighborhood remained much the same as before. Omak walked up the large ornate staircase and entered the sanctuary. Off to the side were the intricate wooden confessionals. An older woman exited the last booth on the right, turned her face to the altar, crossed herself, and left, weeping. Omak had never done the confessional thing; he had explained it to Roslyn by joking that the priest did not want to be there all day. They had laughed. "Oh, sure, you have been such a bad boy!" Roslyn had said, tossing Omak's hair with her hand to emphasize the point.

Omak froze in the main aisleway with the memory. He looked at the empty booth and muttered, "Well, how bad could it be?" He went in, closed the door, and waited. Omak had no idea what form or function of mystic rites he was to employ.

A screen slid to the side a little and a voice said, "Please tell me what troubles you." The answer was more than the priest wanted to know. In the end, after many minutes, the priest slipped a piece of paper through the screen. Upon it was a phone number. The priest told Omak, "I cannot feel the depth of your pain. I cannot condone your actions. From wherever you are after three weeks, call that number. I will not be the one who will answer. They may be able to help you. I cannot. Try to be at peace." And with that the screen slid closed. Omak left with the scrap of paper in his pocket. The priest threw up in the nearest waste receptacle and muttered, "Well, that certainly wasn't divine."

Omak drifted here and there across the Midwest, not following a path. In the meantime, after regaining his composure, the priest opened the church safe and pulled out a small leather folder. In the folder were some sheets of paper; on those sheets were numbers—phone numbers without names. The priest thought for a moment and dialed the seventh number down. There were many clicks and slight bursts of static and then a faint ringing from the opposite end. The phone rang and rang and rang. Anyone else dialing the number would have long since hung up.

After thirty-two rings, the call was picked up. "Yes?" The voice was flat, devoid of accent or life. It sounded like sand pouring through a funnel.

"I, I, well." The priest lost his train of thought, and his voice faded.

From the other end, the voice again said, "Yes?" It had no inflection, it did not sound like it cared one way or the other, and it could have been computer generated for all the priest knew.

"I have run across something, I mean, I have run across someone. Someone who might be useful." The priest looked to the ceiling of the office and gave a silent prayer that he did not sound like a complete fool.

"Yes?"

"I was wondering how to relay the information about what I was told, how do I, you know, communicate the, the, stuff." The priest again looked at the ceiling, hoping that by some miracle at this point he would not be reprimanded for sounding moronic. The fax machine began to hum. The priest turned and thought to himself, in a most undignified manner, *Jesus Christ, now what?* A piece of paper fell out onto the floor, and landed printed side up. On it was an email address.

The voice whispered like the scales of a snake on dry leaves, "Send here." And the phone went dead.

The priest opened the bottom drawer of his desk and produced a bottle of brandy. He fumbled around the desk for a glass for a moment and then said, "Ah, screw it." He pulled the cork from the bottle with his teeth and took two long pulls. So fortified, the priest opened the secret center section of the desk and proceeded to download the video and audio of the man's confession into a file that could be emailed. In minutes it was on its way to, well, the priest thought, to at least someplace. He took another stout drink, recorked the bottle, and leaned back into his chair, cradling the bottle in the crook of his arm. To no one in particular he said, "I have no idea what I have just done." For him, it would be just another mystery about the inner workings of another large corporation, which was ultimately what the Church was.

On the other side of the world, on a state-of-the-art display monitor, an icon began slowly blinking. A withered hand with a thumb and one finger tapped the icon with a yellowed stub. Cigarette smoke filled the air, the ashtray overflowing. The skin was as thin as ancient parchment; veins crossed the back of the hand, patterned like an aerial view of an ancient watercourse. The remains of the fingers had been inexpertly repaired long ago; still, there was an off-colored rawness that decades had not erased.

The file opened and the audio and video began to play. The figure was at first indifferent to the sight and sound. Initially aloof and disinterested the old man was unaffected by what he saw and heard. Yet after the opening sentences, the remains of the human under the robe slowly leaned forward and began absorbing each and every word, as if the content was a tonic, an elixir that brought energy to the dried husk within. Again the voice, like sand, like scales, like ash blown along by a small breeze: "Yes, yes, I feel the pain as well."

Using a stub of a finger, the man pushed a small bell switch once and waited. Within a moment, there was a knock at one of the two doors of the room. The door opened after a respectful pause. "Yes? What is it, sir?" A young man dressed in garb that could be easily mistaken for priestly vestments, lacking only the white collar, stood looking at a point one foot above the top of the older man's head.

Here Palix stood, staring above the old man's head, or where he assumed the head was; the robe's hood was like a peaked ridge that ran back down the old man's neck like an appendage, an exterior spine. A tobacco-stained hand held forth a USB drive. Palix held out his hand palm up and waited for the drive to drop in. He startled when the older man's hand touched his. It was cold, like stone. Dull gray eyes stared from the edge of the robe. The blue-black marks under the eyes indicated days, weeks, and maybe decades of sleep deprivation. The facial skin was almost as translucent as the skin of the hands and wrists. Hundreds of tiny red vessels were etched just under the skin over the whole right side of the face. The skin around the lips was stained a sickly yellow. Palix pulled back in revulsion, the corner of his mouth twitched. "Discover everything." The robed head turned back to the monitor. The exit from the room was for Palix a flight to safety and to the tenuous security of his friends in the outer office.

With the door closed behind him, he looked about the small office. No windows, no carpet, just beige walls and floors and ceiling. From the doorframe of the old man's office the stench of cigarette smoke curled out like a spreading malignancy. Five other men sat staring back at him, questioning, fearful. He straightened his shoulders and pulled himself upright. In two steps, he was at his console nearest the door, where the cigarette stench was strongest. He shook visibly for a moment before sitting down. He pushed the USB drive into his computer and expertly typed a command. The playback of the man's confession began on all the monitors in the room, simultaneously. Without anyone saying a word, facial recognition software was employed, voice stress analysis was engaged, and the man's clothing was minutely examined in every detail. Records checks were made to verify the story of the man who was missing in Chicago, who had just gotten out of jail, to confirm what he had been sent there for, how long ago. In five hours, the six men in the room knew just about everything there was to know about Delano "Del" Omak. Except the key element of how to find him.

The other men in the room sent their files to Palix, the young man by the door. He consolidated the material into an in-depth report, and this he sent into the room that held the old man. New requests for other information popped up almost instantly, many containing audio and video files of people making confessions, being videotaped in private conferences, and being surveyed at their most private moments of contact with the Church. Some Church members used the confessional as a means to exact revenge on other members. This helped the Church maintain its control, through blackmail if necessary. It also helped with investment strategies if some member confessed to embezzlement, stock fraud, or banking irregularities, or disclosed forthcoming earnings reports, stock splits, and more. Information, its gathering or suppression, was vital to the Church and had been for hundreds of years.

From time to time, a request emanated from the old man regarding their mystery man from Chicago. Odd requests.

"Call this banker and request this information."

"Produce a copy of this passport."

"Give this file to this agent."

Nothing seemed to be clicking. Yet all the men in the larger room knew that the old man had a way of seeing into the smallest of things, discovering the thinnest of threads that could be woven into a fabric.

Omak sat outside a fast-food restaurant in Omaha, bored with the road and feeling very lonely. He felt a twinge of anger when he thought of his uncharacteristic impromptu confession. Omak neither felt guilt or remorse; he did, however, feel right about the brutal end of Kent Shelton. Omak had long discarded the slip of paper the priest had given him; he wanted nothing to tie him to Chicago, physically or mentally. That part of his life was over. His disposable cell phone vibrated in his pocket.

He changed phones every two to three weeks; this particular phone was just three days old to him. More often than not, in spite of his repeatedly asking the cell phone providers to do otherwise, he was given a number they had just taken out of service from someone else. Most of the calls he got were for other people, from creditors, friends trying to reconnect using an old number, and once from a hysterical man begging for the return of his true love. Whenever he got a call like that, Omak would drop the phone in the nearest trash can and drive another two hundred miles before getting a new one. His only real purpose for having the phone was to call ahead for motels, gas stations, or directions. He flipped the phone open and said nothing. A small bit of static came through the earpiece and a disembodied voice said, "We know how you feel. Come to us, Delano Omak." The line went dead.

In three strides, Omak was in his car and moving lawfully away from the restaurant. The phone was twisted up in his food wrappers with the battery removed. It now rested in the garbage can in the restaurant parking lot, fading from sight in the rearview mirror. Omak knew from his police career that someone very smart with access to very expensive equipment had spent a lot of time and effort to make that call. Sweat ran down the center of his back and pooled against his skin at his belt line. His right hand opened the center console and he grabbed the grip of his automatic. Comforted by firepower at his disposal, he got on the interstate and headed west.

He waited two weeks before thinking it was all just a bad dream. It had to have been a mistake; he had been too careful. At a strip mall in Casa Grande, Arizona, Omak went into a RadioShack. He was careful to keep his baseball cap pulled low over his eyes. The clothes he wore in Omaha had long since been discarded. He had gone through all of his possessions piece by piece, looking for a bug, looking for something that might have been a tattletale. There was nothing.

One of the employees smiled at him. "Welcome to RadioShack," she said, and then her voice went into warp drive as she recited the current speech about batteries, earphones, or whatever was the hot button item of the quarter. Omak walked by the display of webcams and approached the sales counter. The overhead security cameras sat under small black acrylic covers. One was on a remotely controlled pan-tilt device. It silently swung around to watch Omak. "I'd like a phone, month to month, paid in advance." He pulled some bills from his pocket. The money caught the eye of the sales clerk. She shifted her gaze to the high-priced gadget-filled phones that could translate text messages and surf web pages, decipher bar codes, and play hundreds of games. Omak pointed to a small nearly featureless phone that was cheap.

"What about that one?" he asked.

"Sure, but it doesn't have internet. It doesn't even have a camera or video camera. How will you take pictures of your children and send them to relatives?"

Omak flushed and glared at the girl. "I'll take that phone, if you don't mind."

Fifteen minutes later, Omak was headed north towards Phoenix, with a mind to end up in Las Vegas, when the new phone rang softly. He slowed the car and pulled over onto a service road. Omak stared at the display. It was blank; no caller ID information came through. He flipped the phone open and said nothing. Again there were soft static noises and spans of silence. Again the voice spoke. "We know how you feel. Come to us, Delano Omak. We can give you a life. Not the one you lost. A new life. Not a better one. We cannot do that." There was silence. Omak was lost in thought when a semi driver thought he would be funny and try to get as close to Omak's car as he could and blast the air horn. Omak jumped as the big diesel missed his car by inches, its six-pack of air horns blaring at bumper level.

"What have I got to lose?" Omak said, slightly un-nerved. He calmed himself. "Sure, just one thing."

There was a moment's pause. Omak was unsure if it was respectful or a brief silence granted to the anger of someone important negotiating with an inferior. "Yes?"

Omak went to a mailbox outlet in Kingman, Arizona. As promised, there was a box for him simply addressed to "R and M," care of the retailer's address. The hair on Omak's neck stood up when he looked at the package. There wasn't a shipping label, or any postage, which meant that it had been hand-delivered to the store. Omak shifted his gaze to a spot on the glass display case behind the clerk. He had already decided that the clerk was not a threat; the old gentleman had palsy and looked twenty years past his retirement age. By shifting his stance as if he was intently staring at objects in the display case, Omak could get a fairly good reflective view of the street behind him. There were no cars, no vans, and no doorways to consider; in fact, the road was clear, as was the parking lot. Across the street sat some overgrown commercial land with a faded and barely discernible For Sale sign hanging by one nail. The slight breeze caused the sign to gently flop to and fro. Omak relaxed, placed a twenty on the counter as a tip, thanked the old man, and began to exit the store. Before he got to the swinging front door, he shifted the package to his left hand and dropped his right to a position near the automatic tucked into his waistband under his lightweight vest. A quick glance to the left and right down the sidewalk revealed nothing more threatening than an eight-year-old girl walking towards him. She smiled at him. Omak thought of his daughter for a moment.

The girl stopped beside Omak as he placed the package in the rear seat. She was still smiling at him. He was a little perplexed and turned towards the girl. "Yes, missy, can I help you?"

She smiled even more broadly. "You need to be more careful. They are going to invest a lot in you." With that, she continued down the sidewalk, not even glancing over her shoulder.

Omak felt cold, nearly petrified with fear, for the second time in his life. It was all he could do to get into the car and find a cup of coffee someplace without either laughing hysterically or crying. He had been taught a lesson. It was delivered perfectly. It struck deep and in all the right spots. He found a shady spot near a drive-through and leaned against the driver's door and slowly sipped his coffee. And there was a message within the message: the little girl who had frightened him was wearing the same style of dress that Lacey had been wearing when she died.

"Well," he said to the steering wheel, "I believe I am working with professionals."

He drove further west, ending up in San Diego for a few days. In the quiet of a Sheraton Suites near Copley Symphony Hall, he set the unopened package on the bed. He pulled out the automatic and laid it within easy reach on the quilted bed cover. Omak drew a small knife from his pocket and extended a sharp blade. He placed this next to the gun. He had looked at the package briefly after he got it, but was not inclined to open it until he had driven hundreds of miles in a circuitous route to get to the hotel. It did not smell, leak, or rattle. There was nothing in the way of evidence on the outside of the package to indicate where it had come from. For all Omak knew, the old man behind the counter in Kingman had packaged it.

The knife blade slid between paper and tape easily. Omak proceeded with caution. Soon Omak had a large square of wrapping paper and a cardboard box set out before him on the bed, all of it unremarkable.

"Here's to luck," he muttered. He slid the blade down the centerline between the two flaps of the box. The two top halves sprung open slightly, and to his relief, he was not blown to bits. Omak gently pried the lip of one flap back a little and looked inside with the aid of a small flashlight. All he could see seemed to be filled with solid Styrofoam packing material. Since he did not see any wires or electrical connections or anything out of the ordinary, Omak pulled the top flaps fully apart. Still nothing.

He used the hotel-provided coffeemaker to brew a cup of whatever the establishment provided. Omak sat in a chair and sipped his coffee as he studied the box. Several thought trains had to be evaluated before he felt comfortable in proceeding. If it was a bomb, why not have it go off when he first opened the box? If it was not a bomb, then it didn't matter what he did. He eyed the box and finished his coffee. He rose and stuck his fingers down the sides of the cardboard where it touched the Styrofoam and gently raised the packing material out of the way. He looked inside. There was just a flat surface of more packing material. He took the block he had and looked all over it, thinking he had missed a seam or possibly something embedded in it. It was merely a block of Styrofoam in his hand, nothing more. He slid the lower block out, and again, there was nothing. He took the knife and cut down the seams of the box and studied every square inch of the flattened material. Omak sat back in the chair again and frowned. He grabbed one of the foam blocks and held it near the desk lamp. Slowly, he turned it in every direction, looking for markings, dents, or a cipher that might be useful. Nothing came to light. He repeated the action with the second block, and finding nothing, he minutely examined all the cardboard surfaces of the box. Still nothing.

Omak left the hotel room. It was a Saturday morning, so he toured the Italian market that was held on several blocks of barricaded streets near downtown. He sampled some of the local cuisine and walked aimlessly here and there, following whatever caught his eye. Omak then simply found a street that he liked and walked until he ran into the Pacific Ocean. From there, he caught a cab and went back to the hotel. His room faced west and had a peekaboo view of the ocean out towards the Coronado Bay Bridge. He looked at the door and kicked himself for not putting out the "do not disturb" sign before he had left. Omak pushed the door open with his foot and had his hand ready to draw his gun if something was amiss. The maid had come in while he was out and tided the room, and turned down the bed. She had put the wrapping paper under the box, which was then placed on the desk near the window. Part of the paper flapped slightly in the gentle breeze of the air conditioning unit. This part was backlit by the setting sun over the Pacific. Visible only when fully backlit was what appeared to be part of a number.

Omak grabbed the paper and held it against the window as the last rays of sunshine faded into the ocean. A telephone number appeared and then slowly faded away as the sun slipped beneath the horizon. The phone in Omak's pocket began to softly vibrate. He pulled it out and looked at the number on the screen, then thought back to the number he had seen on the paper. The numbers were the same. Someone was watching him from somewhere, maybe from this very room. He hit the answer button.

"I'm here," he said.

"So are we." It was a different voice than before, a much younger male voice.

Omak waited; it was a trick used by cops, investigators, and news reporters. People always want to talk and will if given the opportunity. Omak waited a little more, and then growing a little perplexed said, "Great! You called me. Congratulations. Are we done yet?" Another cop trick—feign impatience, feign a willingness to draw the conversation to a close.

"I see you are clever enough to figure out the key. You are clever enough to know that you are being watched." Omak's head began to act like it was on a swivel. The smoke detector on the ceiling, was the camera there? Was it in the air conditioning register? Was it in the clock radio beside the bed? There was a small laugh. "Don't worry, Mr. Omak, you should consider that you are always being watched." There was a pause, and then another small laugh. "We hoped you would have found the code earlier today, but no matter, no matter at all." There was a slight pause. "After all, time is always on our side."

Omak listened hard to the voice, seeking information about the caller through his tone, since his words conveyed nothing. It sounded very much like the voice was reading a script and did not want to deviate from it. He felt he was not the first to be so "handled." Omak was actually fine with that; procedures and processes indicate intelligence. Intelligence spawns purpose, and purpose was what Omak wanted most.

———————

Palix Van Trump set the phone down in the cradle and smiled. He had been waiting for a long time, as the Vatican was nine hours ahead of San Diego. Fleetingly, he considered using the late hour as an excuse to put off visiting the cramped and reeking office. Palix had been on the receiving end of the old man's wrath before and did not want to repeat the experience.

The pressing demands of his work load left him little time to ponder his future. In brief snippets of free time he wondered how many years more he would have to languish in servitude before he was allowed to re-enter the mainstream Church. *When, if ever, will I be free?*

———————

The next day, as Omak walked into the hotel lobby after having coffee down the street, the concierge waved him over. "Ah, Mr. Colville, yes?" Omak nodded. There is a package for you. Shall I have it taken to your room?"

Omak thought for a moment, and decided caution was his best plan. "Sure, and thanks." He left a ten on the counter as a reward. Omak took the stairs, giving himself more options for fight or flight. He waited and took some deep breaths on the fifth-floor landing before easing the door into the hallway open. No one was in the hall, and he could use the ornate hallway mirror to look back down the hall behind him. He fully swung the door into the stairwell and walked to his room, keeping one eye on the mirror to check his six. The hallway behind him was deserted. The maid had come and gone, narrowing the potential reasons for someone to approach the door. Omak stood in his room, facing the door.

He heard the elevator chime. Omak was positioned to see the crack under the door and therefore knew when someone was outside his room. His right hand pulled his vest back slightly. There was a knock. Omak looked quickly through the spyglass and saw the bell captain waiting with a delivery held in both hands. With both hands of the bell captain in sight, Omak relaxed a little and craned his neck to get as great a view up and down the hallway as he could. Satisfied, Omak opened the door, said thank you, held out a ten, and closed the door. This package had something in it, and the weight shifted a little as Omak gently moved it to and fro. Since the first had not detonated, he felt reasonably sure this one would not either.

Inside, he found a somewhat odd-looking laptop computer with a collapsed satellite dish. There were two sheets of what appeared to be typed instructions, which contained a picture of the San Diego skyline.

"Typed? Who the hell does that anymore?"

He set the laptop down on the desk and studied the instructions. They were simple and concise. Plug computer into the supplied power strip, place sat dish in window and aim it basically southwest. The skyline picture had a small hand-drawn "x" showing the approximate location that the dish should point to. The directions told him to run a cable from the dish to the laptop and turn the laptop on. Omak did everything except turn the laptop on. He studied the sat dish and the laptop intently. He reached for the "on" button. He stopped and minutely examined the power strip as well.

"Well, here goes nothing." He pushed the button.

It did everything laptops have done for dozens of years. It made whirring noises, various little lights flicked on and off, and the screen went from jet black to a light blue to a welcome screen that had a picture of the lackluster skyline of Cleveland in winter. Omak sat back. "Cleveland? Really?" He looked at the directions again, looked back at the screen and again in disbelief said, "Cleveland?"

It was a nondescript building about six blocks off the National Mall. A tall brick fence surrounded the property. Plants were tied onto espaliers. Ione referred to espaliered plants as "plants in bondage" and disapproved. There was an automatic gate on the street side that led into a small parking area for about a dozen cars. Bey used his cell phone to key in the code that would tell those inside that he was arriving. Even disinterested passersby could easily see the closed-circuit cameras tracking them as they walked down the sidewalk or drove by. These cameras had much larger than normal camera housings. But then the housings also concealed chopped-down versions of miniguns and a nearly endless supply of bullets.

As he walked to the front door, Bey could hear the servos whine as the cameras tracked him. There was a palm reader at the front door, as well as a small camera right at eye level. Bey patiently stared into the lens. Someone was comparing his iris tattoo against the picture they had on file. The door clicked open; the guns did not fire. Bey could see filled and painted-over holes and partially concealed concrete chips by the entrance, reminders of shots fired at someone less lucky.

Bey walked into the reception area where Miss Smith sat politely at her desk. Both of her hands were out of sight. He kept both of his hands in plain sight at all times. Random acts by a visitor could bring ruin.

Bey moved very slowly and only when she told him to. Miss Smith smiled and nodded towards one of the five doors that led into or out of the reception area. Bey himself had only been through three of those doors. The door Miss Smith directed him to was one he had not been through before. When Bey reached for the door, the lock clicked open. He entered a plain and unimposing office. There was a modest desk in about the center of the room with one chair for a visitor in front of it. The desk name-plate said "Mr. Smith."

Everyone he had ever met at this place was named Mr., Mrs., or Miss Smith. Mr. Smith sat behind the desk and was reading what appeared to be Bey's briefing and request. Bey quietly stood near the chair until Mr. Smith motioned for him to sit down.

"Interesting idea. A simple idea. Nature rewards sim-plicity." Mr. Smith placed the paper down and picked up a small sheaf. He briefly checked the top sheet and then handed the stack over to Bey. "I think these documents will help you with the plan you are working on. The peo-ple listed at the bottom of the page are those that have the skills you require and the access to lab space and other facilities that you have detailed. You will find in one of your next messages the names of various private aid organiza-tions and existing United States foreign aid outreach pro-grams that you can use as you deem necessary. Thank you for coming. Nature likes simple things, don't you think?" Bey nodded in agreement.

Bey stood, took the packet, and left, carefully folding the papers and placing them in his breast pocket. As always, he smiled politely at the receptionist; Miss Smith had been replaced by a huge black gentleman, who scowled at Bey. Upon exiting the Smith House, he could feel a trickle of sweat running down his spine. After fifteen years of visiting this place, he always had the same reaction.

On the plane to New England, Bey read intently the papers he had been given. There was a listing of a variety of books, articles, and theses that covered the various aspects of the population problem. Bey's initial list of problem areas around the world had been categorized by the Smiths and ranked in order of importance. Everything south of the Rio Grande was in the first category, followed by areas in the Middle East, the Indian subcontinent, and areas of Asia. Next in the collection of papers was a listing of doctors, religious leaders, chemists, manufacturers, shippers, geneticists, and a smattering of other individuals who might be of use to him. The names with the periods in front of them were the names of contract killers, and generally Bey had to call the Smiths to get permission to employ them. Generally.

Sadly, some of the books were not of the kind that could be easily found online and downloaded to his computer at the Boston airport. Bey zipped a message to the Smiths about this. When he arrived in Portland, Maine, the books had been scanned, and he was able to download the last two on his list of reading he wanted to accomplish.

———————————

With help from his young assistant, the monsignor assembled his plan. Food was quietly secreted away in the basement of the church. Families were advised to collect warm clothing and stout footwear for the trip over the pass to the south. Letters had been written and received, indicating that other churches were ready and able to assist. In fact, there appeared to be some encouraging words about the better treatment of the Jews in the areas they had reached out to. Word spread softly through the village. The Church was there to help them all. The young priest helped to gather and catalogue the food and supplies for the trip. He had elected to stay behind and replace the monsignor and tend to the remaining villagers as best he could. The monsignor argued against this plan as being foolhardy and full of too much unnecessary risk. With difficulty, the younger man stood his ground; not everyone was going to make the trip, and someone had to stay behind and care for the church and the villagers. They prayed together to speed the day when normalcy would return.

———————————

The retired Nobel laureate Dr. Chelan Lucerne lived an hour north of Portland, Maine. Dr. Lucerne's pioneering work on birth control was viewed, depending on one's point of view, as either the salvation of the planet or work spawned in hell. The Smiths had communicated with Dr. Lucerne and told her of Bey's planned visit.

The drive was pleasant; the fall colors were out. The rented Cadillac with the big V-8 engine was fun and responsive. Bey arrived at three in the afternoon. The sun was beginning to hang low in the sky, and the air had a chill to it.

Dr. Lucerne's housekeeper met Bey at the front door and walked him around to the back of the wooden home, generally described as a saltbox. The grounds of the estate were well kept in a natural way. No contrived flower beds, no gravel paths, no fountains with statues of little boys peeing into the water. Squirrels darted amongst the fallen leaves and chased each other here and there.

Dr. Lucerne was raking leaves into a small fire pit. Smoky tendrils rose up on the thermal column and then spread out through the maples and the oaks. Bey was beginning to feel that he was on the verge of stepping into a Currier and Ives painting on a cookie tin. The housekeeper introduced him to Dr. Lucerne, who removed her glove and shook his hand with remarkable strength for a woman of seventy-five.

"So you are the dolt that the Smiths sent up from Washington to talk to me about birth control? Fine. Selah, get us some hot spiced cider and bring it out." Selah turned to the house. "Or would you prefer something more to your liking? Like the blood of a virgin?"

Bey was caught off guard for a moment. "The hot cider sounds fine, and from what I hear there are a lack of virgins over the age of ten in these parts."

Dr. Lucerne smiled. "Yes, do tell." She waved Bey over to a set of Adirondack chairs. "And what questions can I answer for you? I can give you one hour."

She appeared to like directness, so he responded, "I'm not here to save the world. Just our part of it."

Her eyes narrowed, and if she had been a snake Bey would have tried to jump clear of the impending strike. Her eyes relaxed, and she smiled. "Well, that could take more than an hour. Tell me what you have and what you know."

Since the Smiths had placed her on the list, she was safe for Neah to talk to. The slight droop of her eyelids made it difficult to see the tattoo on her iris, if it was there. When it became too dark and cold outside, they retired to her study.

———————

The Sister finished chatting with the priest about a few maintenance issues in the schoolhouse and retired to her small office. Lately, she knew that her mind was wandering. Intense memories seemed to rise out of her thoughts at any given moment. In one flashback, she was dancing in the street at her older sister's quinceañera; guitars were playing loudly in the village square, colored skirts were swirling in the lantern light, and her sister could not have looked more beautiful. She rested her hands in her lap and permitted herself the small pleasure of humming her favorite festival tunes.

There was a soft knock at her door. She knew the priest's knock, and the knocks of the children who came to tattle and see if there was a fresh supply of candy in her drawer. This was a different knock. She rose and steadied herself against the desk. "Yes, please come in."

The door swung open, and there stood a young man she had never seen before. He wore the garb of a priest, but without the white collar. The young man stood at the door and waited politely.

"Yes? Oh, excuse me, please come in."

"Well, Sister, thank you very much." The young man entered the room, carrying a small cube-like suitcase. He pulled the door closed behind him.

"Please have a chair." She motioned to the elderly bit of furniture across from the desk. He noticed the ravages of time on her hands, and imagined how painful it must be for her to perform everyday chores.

The young man sat and slowly extended his hand towards the Sister. "Hello, I'm Palix Van Trump from the Vatican." She accepted his light handshake, fearing that she would get her hand crushed. Sometimes some of the local farmers and children forgot about her arthritis.

"From the Vatican? Here? You must want to see Father Sedro?" She started to rise to lead him to the priest's office on the other side of the sanctuary.

"No, Sister." He softly pulled her hand back to the desk. "I assure you, I have come to see you."

They chatted about everything and anything, from festivals, to church attendance, to the flowers in the courtyard, to the songs of birds on the eaves, to the orphans. The young man was most curious about the orphanage. The number of children needing adoption was down? The number of children showing up from around the village was steadily in decline? Had she heard of other villages experiencing the same thing?

From time to time, the young man referred to a sheaf of papers that he had pulled from the suitcase. After many minutes, he said, "Oh, Sister, please forgive me, I have a gift from an old admirer of yours."

The Sister stammered, "An old admirer? You are trying to flatter me, sir?" A little color rose in her cheeks.

"Yes, Sister, many years ago you played a recital for a cardinal over near the coast. It was several days' walking and riding in an old bus, but you made the trip anyway. The cardinal was impressed, but your admirer was the secretary to the cardinal, and he remembers your playing with great fondness."

The Sister fussed with imaginary things on her desk. "Yes, I remember visiting, and there were many people with the cardinal." She declined to mention a handsome man with penetrating eyes who never smiled. His hand had been bandaged. "I was very young, maybe just nineteen at the time." The Sister's face flushed a little with embarrassment at the memory of her improper thoughts at the time.

"Well, you made a very favorable impression, and I believe that you mentioned to the cardinal that of all things, you liked the occasional cup of tea. The young secretary has now risen to a position of great importance."

He brought out of the suitcase a large thermos, an old-fashioned one with a metal outer shell and a cork for a top. "I follow orders very precisely, Sister, and I would like the honor of having a cup of tea with you while you tell me about the recital."

This brought a great smile to the Sister's face. "Well, it was so long ago, and I have not had a cup of tea in years." While she was speaking, the young man brought out two cups and a small container of sugar cubes and began pouring steaming hot water into the cups. From the recesses of the case, he brought out a small metal container that held two silver tea balls. Into each he scooped some tea leaves. From across the desk, she could smell the tea and the dried orange peel. It was wonderful.

They chatted about the recital as the tea brewed and the aroma wafted about them. "Would you like some sugar in yours, Sister? Just one perhaps?" She nodded, and a small cube began to dissolve into the amber liquid. He stirred the tea with a small silver spoon that looked very old. She thought it looked exactly like a spoon from the tea service the cardinal had used so many years ago.

The cup was warm in her grasp, and she wrapped both hands around it, feeling the heat ease the stiffness. She sipped, and felt the warmth slide across her lips and down her throat. The young man continued to talk about the artwork that he had seen within the Vatican. As she sipped more, the warmth in her throat spread across her chest and shoulders. It was an amazing feeling; it seemed like she was peeling back the years. She sat a little taller in the chair and softly moved her fingers against the cup, playing the song she had played for the cardinal so many decades past. Flashes came before her mind's eye, of her parents, of her hugging her sisters when she left for the convent, and of her helping to birth dozens upon dozens of village children. The young man's voice seemed to drift from the center of her attention. It became more like a murmur at the edge of her awareness, and still it was nice and comforting.

Slowly the warmth crept along her legs and arms until she felt she was standing in the bright sunlight, the warmth of eternity saturating her very being. The sunlight grew until it seemed that she was standing next to the sun itself, without being burned, without being harmed, without feeling fear; her last thought was that God was embracing her.

He waited until her chin gently eased down to her chest and the last of her breath sighed from her. There was a cot in the small office where he supposed she rested from time to time. Gently, he lifted her to her cot. With the tips of his fingers, he closed her eyes. There was a faint smile upon her lips; the pain lines around her eyes had eased. Palix stood beside her and said a prayer. Quietly, after wiping away his tears, he exited the room, softly closing the door behind him. Case in hand, he walked away from the church into the lowland fog. This was just one of many such stops for Palix Van Trump.

He had argued, but to no avail, the old man was adamant. Any and all loose ends had to be secured, at any cost. This knowledge had to be contained.

Another package arrived that contained a brand new digital Nikon camera with every available lens. The next package after that contained a near professional-grade video camera and an array of wireless bugs. The third package contained seventy thousand dollars in small bills. They were crumpled and untidy, as if recently scooped from the offering plates of dozens of churches.

Omak was sure the laptop had been off when he left for a morning walk along the beach, yet now it was proudly displaying the skyline of Cleveland again. He sat down and stared at the screen.

"Well, my little friend, you need to show something better than Cleveland." Omak had barely finished whispering the request when the screen changed to a panoramic view of downtown Pittsburgh. So someone was watching and listening.

He stared at the screen and whispered, "This is not better. I'd prefer to see the skyline of, say, Kingston, Jamaica." The screen flicked and there was Kingston. He then rattled off Miami, Sao Paolo, Gibraltar, and Coventry in rapid succession. There was hardly a delay as each picture sprang to the screen.

At the bottom margin of the screen, a message appeared. Omak's hand edged towards the automatic in his waistband. "You will run out of names before we run out of pictures. Shall we proceed?"

Omak's list of cities amused Palix, and he would have enjoyed playing this little game longer, but there was a cough from the next room. All the young men knew that the old man recorded and monitored their computer activities. A cough or a shout from the cloister was an indication of irritation and was never a good sign. The slightest failings on any account were dealt with immediately and with a vengeance. Fear kept the young men in check; they even called themselves *inmates* in private. A few months ago, one of their fellows incurred the fearsome anger of the old man. Vatican security descended upon the room and dragged the man away. Weeks passed, and a rumor spread that their former comrade had perished of a tropical disease in the Congo River Basin.

Wearily, Palix made himself another pot of coffee and tried to flatten the wrinkles in his shirt with a damp towel. It would be another long day.

Omak's first assignment was to follow and report on the activities of the son of an incumbent liberal state legislator. Legislator Curlew St. John had always been a flamboyant and audacious liberal. It was all an act, as his close friends and associates well knew. He would laugh at very private affairs and shout, "It's just what sells today! Tomorrow, I might have to reinvent myself as a Palinite!" He then would take a huge gulp of whatever was in his glass and shout again, "Gawd ferbid!" St. John had curried the favor of stars and liberals all around Los Angeles. He and his staff were adept at getting him invited everywhere a camera or a sound bite opportunity might present itself. While most of his fellow Democrats avoided him, finding him unbearably rude and basically ill-mannered, they did have to grant him his ability to sit next to anyone who ever appeared on the cover of *People*. And they, like the emperors of old, knew only too well that it's what the masses want that counts most, not necessarily what makes sense or what is right.

Curlew's wife had long since fled his rude behavior, but not before giving him a son. Carson St. John, age twenty-four, was little like his father. He was quiet, rarely spoke out, and was a mean drunk. On more than one occasion, Curlew had had to call upon friendly police and prosecutors to not bring Carson to task for public drunkenness and fighting. Lately, Curlew's staff had politely suggested that Carson take an extended vacation until after the election, say to someplace either in the Middle East or, possibly, Greenland. Curlew waved his hand impatiently and shouted, "Ha! The boy's growing his wings, and maybe his balls! Let him feel his oats for a while!" The staff simply made sure there was contingency money in various accounts to buy off whomever Carson insulted or assaulted next.

Carson had lived under the immense shadow of his raucous father his whole life. There weren't any pictures of just Carson; there were only pictures of Carson standing slightly behind his father. Even if Carson received an award he had rightfully earned, it always seemed to be handed to Curlew for the picture taking. Carson St. John wanted to make his own mark on the world, make his own money, and make his own way. In concert with some friends, he embarked on creating child pornography.

As pressure within the United States increased to snuff out child porn, it forced Carson and his cabal of friends to pursue new talent in Asia and South America. Money talks, and in poverty-stricken areas, money talks loudly. The cabal's philosophy: a few children here, a few pictures there, some money exchanged, no harm done. Neighbors sold out neighbors, siblings sold out siblings, aunts and uncles sold out nieces and nephews, and even parents could be enticed to spare a few moments of a child's life.

Carson stood in front of a mirror from time to time, practicing his speech. "Think of the good the money will do." He worked very hard not to smile, or just outright laugh, at the gullibility of some people.

Money flowed in. Carson gained a new car, a new apartment; he wanted more. Greed and avarice ruined great men, and Carson couldn't be confused with great men. He studied which of the numerous websites scored the most hits. He studied the content of those sites. Clearly, the more violent and shocking the material, the greater the cash flow.

At the next meeting of the pornographers, Carson produced a new business plan. It would be high end, high dollar, limited access, and generate lots of money. Carson waved the concerns off with his hand, just like his father.

"Hell, there's lots of kids. And they haven't refused the

money yet, have they?" He smiled and produced some sketches and a rudimentary computer presentation. "Who's got the balls to jump in with me?"

They went to Canavieiras, between Salvador and Porto Seguro on the east coast of Brazil. Canavieiras was an isolated fishing and farming village that had fallen on desperate times. Overfishing had decimated the ocean industry. Rampant slash and burn had destroyed the jungle. Any hope for tourism would have to wait a millennium until the jungle crept back. Most families had one or more family member working in distant mines or on farms so far away that it would take days to walk there.

Canavieiras sat at the beginning of Brazil's highway BA-001, near its intersection with highway BA-274. Rio Canavieiras divided the area into basically thirds, with nameless tributaries further chopping the village and surrounding areas into smaller chunks. The runway for the small airport was on the highest point of land in town, a mere sixteen feet above sea level. Flooding in the rainy season was always a problem. On more than one occasion, the villagers carried their meager possessions to the airport and huddled under tarps, leaves, garbage can liners, or garbage can lids to fend off the monsoon as the river slopped through the village.

Carson had done his research on Canavieiras with a measure of competency. Commercial flights to the airport: zero. They would have to fly in to Salvador or Porto Seguro and hire a van to haul the video gear. He selected a hotel that at least had a review. While the review was at best marginal, the other hotel had unwisely posted a picture of its lobby.

Carson St. John's group always had good success when they set up bogus free medical clinics, often masquerading as members of UNICEF or the Red Cross. A cheap color printer and a laminator gave them instant official-looking pocket credentials anywhere they went. Hidden cameras recorded everything in graphic detail. "Doctors" performed "examinations." Ignorant parents, unfamiliar with anything other than rudimentary medicine, drank free sodas and ate sweets in the lobby while loud Latino music blared incessantly. The music masked the cries of the children at the other end of the building. Parents who appeared fidgety were given small sums of money as a reward for participating in some groundbreaking health-care-sponsored study.

Back in the U.S., the marketing arm of the business was in high gear. Special messages were distributed to clients telling them that something was coming that they would not want to miss out on. Snippets of the South American films were flashed across customers' screens. The buy-in was twenty-five thousand dollars. Cash or credit or PayPal, it did not matter. The long green rolled in.

Carson and his favorite photographer, Menlo Prindle, were running a game within a game, a game that would make them rich. They had studied the logins and hits on the websites with an absolute devotion to finding out what would sell. The more a child screamed, the greater the take. If there was blood, the hits went up faster than they could calculate. Prindle watched the data stream.

"Man, there are a lot of sick bastards out there, you know?" Prindle's false scowl eroded into a smirk.

Carson shot Prindle a semi-serious glance. "You mean there are a lot of sick rich bastards out there, you know?"

They both laughed.

It took only a little more money to convince a set of parents that one child needed to remain in the clinic overnight. The next day, as he and Prindle had planned, Carson St. John brutally murdered the child. Carson did this while he wore a clown mask, simply because his research showed that irony was good for business. The two men made eight hundred and seventy-five thousand dollars in two days. The corpse was thrown without ceremony or remorse into a drainage ditch south of Canavieiras on the way to the airport.

Two weeks after returning to L.A., they celebrated with champagne and caviar and some high-priced whores.

"How did you make it look so real?" someone asked.

Carson and Menlo laughed.

"Because it was real," Carson said simply. Knowing that the murder might not be well received, Carson and Menlo had come prepared with a paper grocery sack. A few of the group looked very unhappy until Carson and Menlo handed out bundles of money—fifty thousand dollars to each member of the cabal. Carson knew that this was just the start of something really good.

———

The body of the tiny child was brought to the church shortly after it was found. The priest was also the doctor, the schoolteacher, the veterinarian, the mortician, and more. He cried as he wiped the filth and blood off of the child. As he was straightening the little fingers to clean them, a scrap of plastic fell out onto the makeshift table covered with an old blue plastic tarp. He turned it over and over in his hands.

———

The bit of plastic had made it very nearly around the world and back. And now it sat on Omak's hotel desk in Altadena, California. It was the microscopic examination of that plastic and the arrogance of Carson St. John that would bring about his ruin and that of his father. The Church spared no expense in using every resource at its disposal to support Delano Omak. Files were transmitted to Omak on a regular basis. The most damning was airport surveillance footage of Carson striding through the airport at Porto Seguro, his phony ID hanging off his shirt pocket. He liked it when people thought he was a doctor or a humanitarian. It got him better seats at the bar and the occasional attention of women who normally found him disgusting and rude. A corner on his badge was missing. Omak turned the corner over and over in his fingers.

Omak began asking questions of his computer, knowing full well that a human at the other end was involved. Somehow, he felt better thinking he was just talking to a machine and not another human being. Somehow, it was better to be disconnected, remote, and removed. Palix was on call no matter what the time of day to receive communications from Omak, and to be the conduit for information requested by him. Palix carried a small netbook with him at all times at the old man's insistence.

Omak typed in a question on the laptop. "What are my available resources?"

The answer flashed on the screen. "Unlimited." Omak sat back and thought for a moment. On his morning walk,

Omak had sat at a bus stop and written several cryptic pages of possible avenues he wanted to pursue. He had then gone to an independent coffee shop and scribbled some more while he enjoyed a latte. This had brought a pang to his heart; morning coffee was something he and Roslyn had enjoyed on Sundays before Lacey arrived.

He pulled the small paper notebook from his vest pocket and laid it beside the laptop. He entered two dozen individual items, hitting "enter" after each one. When finished, he tore the notepaper into many small pieces and flushed them down the toilet.

Omak's intelligence and his methodical way of pursuing leads amazed Palix. On the one hand, it made Palix's life easier; on the other, the added work of ferreting out Omak's requests did not diminish his already staggering workload.

The screen saver had kicked in, so Omak had to wiggle his finger on the touch pad to bring back his prior work. As he watched, words began to appear below each of his entries in a different font. Most were simple replies, such as "Two weeks," which was the reply to his request for information on all of Curlew and Carson St. John's banking activities for the past several years. He had asked that the data be sorted by date, sender, and recipient. Omak also asked that Carson's internet operation be investigated to the fullest and asked for the locations of the servers, the names of the users, and the numbers of the accounts. He wanted IP addresses, names, physical addresses—everything that could be gleaned. The response to the request for this information was "Two months." The rest of his requests were fairly straightforward and would be fulfilled in a few days to a week. When the laptop went black, Omak felt focused, invigorated, like when he was a cop narrowing the investigation down from "who could" to "who did."

Thousands of miles east of California, across a continent, the Atlantic, and part of the Mediterranean, the husk of a man under a robe stared intently at his screen. He pushed the bell and the same young man as always appeared, staring, as always, over the top of his head. The withered hand produced another USB drive. The younger man nodded and exited. For a moment, the hooded head bobbed in affirmation of something—possibly something good, or possibly something otherwise. A cigarette was lit and smoldering in the ashtray. The old man did not take the filterless stub to his mouth. Instead, he took out a wood rasp and began to slowly file the raw and bleeding ends of his stumps.

All those years prior, the Germans had been thorough and methodical. After the young priest lost his fingers, the commandant took the list of names from his bloodsplattered shirt. The priest vainly tried to retrieve it and was knocked to the floor. When he regained consciousness and crawled to the basement, he discovered that the Germans had assembled the villagers according to the list in his pocket and shot them all.

With the rasp in hand, he drew it across the stub of one finger. "For Anton." Another stroke across the next stub. "For Bruno." "For Claudette." He recited the names on those on the list in the order in which they had been killed.

———

Back in the main office, Palix stood with the USB drive in his hand. The five other men stared at him silently. They knew from experience that it was far better to wait than to ask. The nearest man's upper lip curled back in revulsion; this expression soon spread to the rest of them. Palix didn't understand the appearance of disgust on his coworkers faces. He twisted the USB in his fingers, suddenly nervous. Something was sticky on the USB; he looked down to see blood dripping from his fingers to the floor. Placing the USB on the desk, Palix quickly ran to the small sink at the back of the room and washed his hands a dozen times.

After he drank a cup of strong black coffee, Palix used multiple sheets of folded paper towels to wipe down the USB before inserting it into his console. The group began to employ larger and larger portions of the Vatican's computer system.

———

A message flashed on the old man's computer. An underling working on some aspect of the system several blocks away had become irate that his work was being pushed further and further back in the queue. The message was threatening at worst, and insulting at the very least. The robed head nodded and laboriously began typing a message to one of his equals at the pope's elbow.

Within minutes, the angry clerk's computer began saving all of its current work. The clerk pounded on the keyboard and said a variety of things not normally heard in the inner recesses of the Vatican proper. The computer shut down, and in spite of the clerk's every effort, it would not restart. As he tried to use the mouse, hammered at the keyboard, and unplugged and plugged in the desktop, a heavy hand descended on his shoulder. There were the Swiss Guards, who did have a role in security, and then there were the plain-clothes officers. Tourists at the Vatican never saw the inner perimeter of anything important, anything about the machine that was the Church. Another set of hands pulled the startled man to his feet; he stammered, "Che cosa? What? Che cosa?" He was whisked away to an office deep under a building four blocks from St. Peter's Square. In polite circles it was an office; everywhere else it was a holding cell. It would be some time before he would reappear. Such was the power of the old man.

———————————

From time to time, Omak checked on the progress of his information requests. He became very impressed with the speed and thoroughness of the data supply. Smiling, he thought about his old friends in Chicago who would sell their souls for…

He stopped. He sat back and finally understood that he had indeed sold his soul. Delano "Del" Omak never smiled again in his life.

Far away, a supercomputer crunched data, made and broke connections, and began building a weapon. Not a bomb, a knife, or a gun, but a weapon of information, irrefutable in its accuracy. Omak watched as the file that was to become the weapon was assembled. In its simplicity, computer code was nothing more than symbology taken to an extreme measure, the universe boiled down, refined, ground into ones and zeroes.

Palix and his team had to work for many days without a break to complete the task in the time frame the old man had prescribed. The sun never sets on the Church. They consumed more resources in just a week or two than some entire countries did over the course of a year. They began the laborious task of assembling the information into a cascade. The cascade birthed one event that, when opened, spawned another event, and another and another. Each segment of the cascade had to be crafted to come from a source remote from the source of all other segments. Each segment had to stand alone.

Curlew St. John felt very good about the coming election. In Curlew's estimation he was running against a paper tiger—someone who is outwardly powerful but inwardly weak—that the Republicans had coerced into running. The Republicans wanted to at least save face by having a candidate rather than simply conceding the election to St. John again.

Lynden Liberty was the Republican candidate for the state seat in Sacramento currently held by St. John. Liberty had the right name to be a candidate for the elephants, and very little else. He had been a party faithful for years, performing each of his political tasks with a measure of attention to detail. When it came to stapling campaign signs together in his small apartment, Liberty was the best. He could do hundreds over the course of a weekend. While St. John was boisterous and dramatic, Liberty was reserved and utterly devoid of attitude and drama. He had no close friends, no family that anyone knew about or ever heard him mention. Liberty showed up early and stayed late, never complained, and never missed an opportunity to help. Local Republican politics was his life outside of working for a multinational accounting firm.

Lynden Liberty had his own office, and while not a corner office, it did mean he had clout. As the supervisor for a group of "fixers" in the firm, Liberty directed the repair of bad corporate credit. He created words and documents that indicated that things were looking up for a person or a company that had fallen on hard times. Liberty on more than one occasion was called upon to suggest how a company should be fixed. Sometimes he would suggest, politely, that certain processes be installed and adhered to. Other times he would simply take the company roster and draw lines through names of people who had to go. Liberty never read the obituaries out of fear that someone he had crossed out had been terminated in a manner more violent than simply being shown the door.

Lynden Liberty had worked for years to be in the right spot at the right time, and now was the spot and now was the time. The local Republican caucus called him into a very private meeting and laid out their plan. They told Liberty that they were going to run a campaign with no money and little chance of victory, but they needed someone to suck it up and be the candidate in a sure-to-fail race. Liberty nodded his head in acceptance and thought for a moment.

"How do we run a campaign with no money? Isn't that like giving up before the first bell of the first round of the fight?" he asked.

There were some uncomfortable looks around the room, and finally the chairman said, "Well, maybe we can come up with some money. What do you think will give us a good show?"

"Oh, I think a few hundred campaign signs, a billboard, ten radio spots, a TV commercial or two." Liberty put his hand to his cheek and thought for a moment longer. "I'd say about twenty-five to thirty-five thousand dollars ought to make it right. I would suggest the higher end of that range, to make a reasonable and responsible show."

It was the chairman's turn to think. He took a face-poll around the executive committee. No one was immediately having a heart attack, so he said, "You've got thirty-five grand. Make us proud, Liberty."

Liberty gave a thin smile and thought to himself, *You fat, stupid asshole, I assure you I am going to make a lot of people like me proud.*

There was one thing about Liberty that neither his company nor the Republican Party knew.

Omak called upon his laptop to begin the implementation of the hard side of the equation. The soft side was all done, and nicely bundled into numerous electronic packages. Each of these packages had a mission; each had a kickoff date. The missing link was the delivery system that had to be executed perfectly from near and far. Each segment of the equation was designed to be just a small part in a net that would ensnare Curlew and Carson St. John. Omak did not dwell on the control of damage beyond his mission. He did not care. What rose from the destruction of the St. Johns was not his concern.

The first tickle of something being amiss came from Australia. It was nearly insignificant, but when studying urban legends, it the generally accepted rule was that a story had to begin in an English-speaking country; this gave the story a measure of credibility at the starting gate. A small tabloid with a circulation of about five thousand people claimed to be in receipt of information implicating a legislator in the United States of involvement in child pornography. The tabloid had a website, and the number of hits that it got the week after the release of the story was five times its weekly average. This was a stupendous increase, as the number of website hits had averaged a dismal two per week over the previous year. It was a start.

A web search alert chirped on a desk that was crammed into a space scarcily more than a broom closet at MSNBC. A summer intern who was headed back to college in three weeks clicked the related icon and began to read. From three thousand miles away, a computer locked onto that mouse click and began rewriting code on the laptop in the broom closet. The intern dismissed the story and was ready to erase it when another icon began blinking. She clicked that and read. Then another, and another, and another.

Computers began trickling information out in text messages, faxes, and emails to charities, to law enforcement, to INTERPOL, to newspapers.

The senior admin threw open the door to Curlew's office just as Curlew engulfed the breast of another staff member with his mouth.

The admin shouted, "Get dressed and get out!"

Curlew wiped the drool off his face and shouted back, "I am gonna kick your skinny black ass all the way back to Torrance!"

This did not deter the admin, who flung a stack of papers down on St. John's desk. "Shut up you dumbass honky motherfucker!"

The female aide had managed to tuck herself back into her blouse and was at the door when the admin shouted after her, "And close the fucking door, bitch!"

St. John stared at the papers; the stack was made up of a disgusting collection of images of children being tortured, molested, and much worse.

"What's this all about? What's this got to do with me?" St. John was reaching for a small revolver he kept taped inside the knee well of his desk.

The admin shouted across the desk, forcing St. John to

roll his chair back two feet. "I told you to watch that son of yours! I told you to send him away!"

St. John stared blankly at the pictures, confused, angry. "What does this have to do with Carson? What does this have to do with me?"

The admin threw another stack of papers on the desk; this stack detailed hundreds of banking transactions that clearly linked the child porn websites to Carson and to Curlew.

The admin sat heavily in a chair across from Curlew St. John, Democratic incumbent and candidate for the state legislature. "This is Carson's company, this is Carson's work. It's all over the web by now. We have shut the phones down. I have told the staff to go home and wait until we call them."

St. John sat back. "Oh, I'm sure a little money here and there will make this go away by tomorrow afternoon."

The admin looked across at St. John. "Well, good luck with that. Tell me how it turns out. The bank accounts have been frozen. We have been told search warrants have been issued for your house, the summer place in Tahoe, Carson's apartment, and his company's headquarters."

In the distance, a loud pounding could be heard at the office entry doors. "And I'm guessing they have a search warrant for here as well." Tires screeched to a halt outside the two-story campaign headquarters building. St. John rose and looked out the window. Outside, CNN, FOX, NBC, CBS, and ABC were pulling up with their remote satellite feed vehicles. Two reporters were having a pushing contest to see who could stand in front of the "St. John, He's Good For YOU!" banner that spanned a third of the building's front.

When he had had his fill of the view, he turned back to address his admin, who was nowhere to be seen. The bookcase had been pushed back to reveal the private stairs that led to the adjacent building, where Curlew kept an apartment and a car. He closed and locked his office doors and returned to his custom-made chair, his throne. It was a large chair that had to withstand his corpulence. The remote lay on his desk, and with that he called up ten television monitors, which flickered to life. Being egotistical and arrogant, he liked having tapes of his interviews played in ten different ways from ten different news sources while he negotiated some bits of legislation with fellow Democrats. It demonstrated clout, and he used it to intimidate his rivals.

Today, there were ten different stories of law enforcement breaking up a massive child pornography ring that had raked in twenty-nine million dollars in the last six months. It showed a ruffled Carson St. John being led away in handcuffs from his apartment. A stone hurled from the crowd caught him on the lip, tearing open a gash that bled down his face and onto his shirt. "Serves you right, you bastard!" Curlew St. John shouted as he stared at the spectacle, while he listened to the front lobby doors disintegrate under a battering ram.

At one of the news stations, some minimum-wage video archivist had unearthed an old interview with Curlew St. John where he said, "Child molesters and rapists should be castrated, beaten, then hung for their crimes!"

Within seconds, all the other channels had copied or found the clip and were playing it over and over again. The doors to Curlew's office burst open, and a tidal wave of police, sheriffs, and highway patrolmen stormed the office, followed by wave after wave of microphone-waving reporters and cameramen pushing and shoving each other. They shouted questions; they bellowed orders. Lights blazed on a dozen video cameras. Flash attachments from many digital cameras lit up the office in staccato bursts of light. As if short-circuited from the excitement, Curlew pointed the remote at the officers and shouted, "Get out or I'll shoot!" as he jumped to his feet.

Curlew St. John, candidate for the state legislature in Sacramento, was ahead in the polls by such a large margin that the election no longer had news appeal to anyone. The election was only slightly more than one week away, leaving the Democrats far too little time to find another candidate, much less to tackle the legal issues associated with trying to stop the election. Curlew St. John was struck fourteen times by bullets fired by officers from several jurisdictions and was dead before he hit the floor.

––––––––––

Carson St. John's fate was far, far worse. He lost everything, and went to prison for life. Child molesters are not treated kindly behind bars, child murderers even less so. Carson's fellow inmates were particularly unpleasant individuals.

––––––––––

Lynden Liberty was going to be elected to the state legislature in Sacramento. He shook hands, signed autographs, and had his picture taken hundreds of times in the week before the election. It did not bother him one tiny bit that his rival had been gunned down on international news. During a private moment, he went to his small apartment and opened up his closet. He sat in a chair after turning on the light and tried to figure out which dress he was going to wear at the inaugural ball. It would have to be something dignified, he thought. The one thing about Lynden Liberty that neither his company nor the Republican Party knew was that Lynden Liberty was transgender.

The press used its combined weight and clout to bring down two U.S. senators, a governor, several police officers, and a state prosecutor, and ruined dozens of marriages, destroyed companies, and more when they began publishing the list of those involved with and who had accessed the websites of Carson St. John. Menlo Prindle was released on bail pending trial. One evening, he went for a drive and never returned.

Omak stared at the laptop; there was a message in an odd old font. It said, simply, "Good." It had taken a year and four months to destroy the St. Johns. Omak was tired, tired into his bones. For a moment he looked at himself in the mirror. He had gray hair and looked gaunt, worn out. He could not remember the last time he had worked out or gone for a run. Omak reached for the computer to turn it off, and to place a thick towel over it. This was his way of signifying to his handlers that he was off the hook for a while. Before he could reach the towel, a message appeared. "Important assignment, rest two days. You will be contacted." He collapsed onto the bed and slept.

Thousands of miles away, Palix Van Trump sat back in his chair and watched as Omak placed a covering over the computer. That was just fine with Palix. The only time he had off was when Omak collapsed from exhaustion and covered the computer. The rest of the indentured men directed appreciative nods of their heads towards Palix, along with the occasional awkward smile.

Omak uncovered the computer, and it sprang to life. He wondered what it would be like to be stuck under a towel for three days; he got his answer on the screen. "You are late."

Somewhat put out, Omak typed back, "Do you wish to replace me?"

The computer sat there for several moments, and then a message appeared: "No." A single icon began blinking on the screen, then another, and another, until half the screen was covered with icons, all numbered. Omak scrolled the mouse around, watching in a disinterested manner as the mouse lit up each icon for a moment, before he moved on. All the icons appeared to be the same; it was only a matter of the numbers attached to each that made them different. Omak randomly selected an icon and clicked on it. It brought up a picture of Neah Bey.

It took Omak three days to read all the material just in the briefs about this mystery project. While it smacked of CIA, NSA, NSC, FBI, and all the rest of the federal government alphabet, there were only wisps and tendrils of pathways and power chains that connected details to the government, nothing concrete. There was nothing anyone other than a very devout conspiracy theorist would attach any meaning to. Omak spent much time walking and rebuilding his stamina; he enrolled in a national gym chain and began to crisscross America by car, by bus, by plane, and by train.

He asked for and received a special Wi-Fi USB connection that allowed him to crack into any attainable connection, undetected. He haunted fast-food restaurants and coffee shops with free internet connections. Omak was more background clutter than anything else once he freed himself of the sat dish. He understood that with the sat dish he was free of many security concerns. Without it, he just had to be a little more discreet and more cautious when it came to people looking over his shoulder. It took some doing at times, to find places that did not have windows through which a passerby could see his work, and he was always checking his six for reflective display cases, shiny surfaces, and glass mounted art and pictures. And he always kept a weather eye for security cameras.

The Church provided Omak with access to unlimited resources. Omak at first was confused as to where to begin in his search for information. Then, like an apparition from his past, the cop in him came forth. "It isn't about the *what*," his father would say. "It's about the *who*."

Omak surveyed the pictures he'd been sent of the odd-shaped building in Washington, D.C., that was more fortress than office. The street-level shots had been taken by

Church operatives, as calling up Google street-level shots of the address yielded random pictures of vacant buildings and old apartment houses. He looked over the pictures and saw the gun ports disguised as ornamental building features. Clearly, there was something a lot more sinister in the closed-circuit television camera housings than mere cameras. Using a magnifying glass, he guessed that each "camera" held approximately two thousand rounds of ammunition. He could just barely read the plaque at the gate, "Smith, LLC." Nothing with that name came up on any search engine he could think of. The two men who patrolled the front door and attended to the remarkably few visitors were obviously armed, and looked like heavy hitters. "Heads on swivels," Omak muttered. It was cop talk for highly paid and highly skilled personal protection details for visiting heads of state and some Hollywood superstars. Omak had seen this type of security personnel before, in Chicago when the vice president came to town; these guys acted just like the Secret Service, always in motion, always looking.

Still, he had to find out if the security was for show or for real. He drove to D.C. and assembled a satchel charge from the materials that were waiting for him at the hotel. A few days of hitting bars and strip clubs brought him in contact with some lowlifes who would be cannon fodder for his experiment. He hired two drug addicts who were at least capable of standing upright and taking simple orders. First, Omak supplied them with several days' worth of amped-up drugs that made them more pliable in terms of doing his bidding. After a few days, he stopped showing up. The withdrawal pangs set in, and his two new friends were very eager to reconnect with him.

"Okay, one more time, I am here to scare that bitch ex-wife of mine a little, no big deal. She is staying at this place right here." Omak showed them a picture of the Smith, LLC building. "All I want you to do is storm the front doors at three in the morning, ring the bell, and run away." Omak nodded towards Colfax, who had been an athlete a long time ago. Tokio was pretty much brain damaged and had to wear slip-on shoes since he lacked enough brain cells or memory to attempt the overly complicated art of tying bows in shoelaces.

"Tokio, old buddy, all I want you to do is throw this backpack of divorce papers over the brick wall, about right here." He tapped a sketch of the brick wall that fronted the street. "Easy as can be, you'll be in and out, over and done, and back here to get your reward." Omak held open his coat and showed them a Baggie filled with some pink-hued powder. Before they got any ideas about killing him in the bar, Omak said, "And this is only part of your payment. The rest comes in tomorrow night after you are done. I meet the courier right here." From another pocket he took out a much smaller Baggie and said, "Here, live it up for a while, and be sure you are there at three." He had to repeat the directions five times, until even Tokio got it right.

He had rented an apartment that had a view of the target building from ten blocks away. The leaves had not quite budded out enough for them to obscure Omak's view of the place. Incredible magnification brought the whole front of the building into crystal clear view. Omak checked his watch. It was 2:58 a.m. He looked back through the Celestron binoculars mounted on a tripod. Hung below the binoculars was an equally impressive video camera with night vision enhancements. It hummed along quietly. Omak saw Colfax and Tokio approach the gated area. They stopped and looked inside. The cameras were already swinging towards them when Colfax mustered his strength and vaulted over the fence. Tokio began running and stumbling towards his assigned spot. Colfax made it to the front door before the first minigun spun up and spewed a five-foot tongue of flame out of its camera housing. Two more guns joined the spray. Tokio's head spun as he was startled when the rapid buzzing chainsaw noise assailed his ears. It was all the old addict could do to throw the backpack over the wall. It landed in the flowerbed just over the fence. Colfax went down in a heap on the front steps. The miniguns stitched across his corpse a few times, just to make sure. Tokio was to the corner when part of the wall opened up. Two men, then three, and finally four jumped out of what appeared to be nothing more than the corner pillar of the wall. In mere seconds, Tokio was knocked down and carted from view. The panel closed and Tokio was never seen again. The backpack blew up. It was not really intended to be destructive. Omak was a little dazzled by the flash of the black powder charge.

Omak quickly gathered the tape from the camera and fled. He had seen the false cupola on the roof peel back and an impressive array of sensors jut into the night sky. Later, on board a flight to Miami, Omak played the tape over and over again. From the time Colfax cleared the fence until Tokio disappeared, thirteen seconds had elapsed. Omak frowned and mouthed the word *Pros*. It was not lost on Omak that the Smiths had considerable firepower and were willing to use it a mere seven hundred yards from where the president and the first lady slept.

At his layover in Miami, Omak searched the local print and electronic news media. Not one word was mentioned about anything unusual occurring in D.C. the night before. "Okay, no frontal assault is going to work without more planning," he said to himself.

Omak began looking through one of his lists. This particular list was a compilation of the world's best and brightest geneticists, leaders in birth control, and scientists who had ever said anything about overpopulation being the next worst thing coming down the highway for humanity. One name popped up in all three categories: Dr. Chelan Lucerne from New England.

It was a cozy room, lined with bookshelves, with a gas fireplace that warmed the air as well as the spirit. Selah was instructed to bring them a snack around five, and then coffee and a small piece of cake at seven.

In the end, Dr. Lucerne told Bey that there were a variety of excellent methods to prevent sperm 'A' from fertilizing egg 'B.' All you needed was a method that was acceptable to the population under scrutiny. They chatted about pills, shots, sterilization, patches, and abstinence. The last option seemed the least likely. Dr. Lucerne described each topic in detail. It was as if Bey had gone back forty years or more, to some junior high school physical education class on human reproduction, except this instructor was a sharp-witted gray-haired scientist and not some red-faced coach trying not to tell grubby adolescent boys dirty sailor stories. To this day, Bey remembered more of the dirty sailor stories than he did any other part of the coach's speech or the horrific movie about sexually transmitted diseases. Bey wondered what was in the movie that they showed the girls in his school. The girls avoided speaking to the boys for two weeks afterward.

Here were the means; as Dr. Lucerne described it, all they had to do was develop the delivery system.

Bey stayed over in Portland, and in the hotel room read through some of the book synopses that the Smiths had sent. There was any number of voluntary methods to reduce the birthrate. Courts and governments typically ordered the involuntary ones. The Chinese had been only marginally successful at enforcing the one-child-per-household rule.

A number of pie charts and graphs indicated that the lower the average number of years of education and the lower the standard of living, the greater the respective birthrate. As Dr. Lucerne put it, "That's the true definition of being *fucking stupid*. No education, no job, what else ya' gonna do?" Bey flushed a little red at the crude remark, which made the good doctor chuckle for several minutes.

There were a number of groups trying to raise the standard of living and increase the education of the populations that Bey was targeting. In reality, their efforts only made the situation worse for the people they were trying to help. The local populations were torn apart and confused once they understood that they lived in a shit hole and could do nothing about it. They also understood that with a slightly higher standard of living and education, they lived longer to appreciate their dismal existence over a greater length of time. It occurred to Bey that if each country, race, or religion just took care of its own house, it would not have the time to ruin anybody else's. However,

Bey knew that was never going to happen. Intelligence is fleeting. Bey frowned.

Bey read through more material on the flight home. His wife picked him up at the airport, and they had a light snack of items picked up at the Metro Market before retiring. The next morning, Bey awoke, did his exercises, and had an espresso with Ione. They had been married for nearly thirty-five years, and never once had Ione complained about his peculiar career path, the travel, or the fact that sometimes he came home from a conference with stitches, a limb in a cast, or suffering from some tropical parasite.

Omak headed towards Maine. He had the terrain scouted and mapped. A number of items were sent to him at a general delivery drop at the post office. He waited in a small pie and coffee place north of Portland for the sun to rise a little higher in the sky. He was decked out in bird-watching gear, with an alpine-style hat, a walking stick that could double as a monopod for his binoculars, a herringbone jacket, and some REI cargo pants. He had a small camouflaged backpack riding across his back. A copy of a Roger Tory Peterson field guide stuck out of one of his pockets. He set out in the morning, following fairly closely the directions the local Audubon Society had given to him at the library the day before. Some feathered friends were on an annual migration from someplace over there to someplace else to the southeast.

Omak followed the main road, occasionally stopping and using the binoculars to spy on something in the trees. In about forty-five minutes, he came to an overgrown logging road and headed southwest through the forest.

Omak stopped and leaned up against a tree and studied his satellite imagery and the provided map. Dr. Lucerne's house was about a hundred and thirty yards away. He began to slowly pick his way through a thicket. When he was ten yards off the path, he knelt down and began undoing the backpack. In minutes, he had transformed himself into something nearly invisible in the failing light. The ghillie suit had been custom made. Omak began a laborious crawl and wait and crawl routine, progressing slowly towards Dr. Lucerne's house. A squirrel or chipmunk bounded in front of him so closely that he jerked, thinking he was going to feel teeth and claws; however, the little critter just darted away into the leaf clutter on the ground. The damp cold of the Maine forest made the hours long and exhausting. At thirty yards, he pulled out his small set of binoculars and watched Dr. Lucerne rake some leaves into a small fire pit. The smoke rose and fanned out through the trees. He slowly reached for the automatic under his arm. Omak froze as another much younger woman escorted a man into the backyard. Omak frowned. The man was Neah Bey. Bey and Dr. Lucerne chatted for a while at the fire and then edged their way to some rough-cut wooden lawn furniture nearer the house. Bey continued to speak with Dr. Lucerne, but his head never stopped moving, like it was on a gimbal. Omak ever so slowly flattened himself out against the ground and waited until darkness filled the area and Bey and Lucerne had entered the house. He waited for an additional thirty minutes to elapse and then, with just as much trepidation as before, drifted through the trees like the last remnants of the smoke.

Joyce was out jiggling again, so Bey waved to her across the yards. He could hear Ione whisper through the screen door, "You pervert."

Joyce started hanging up clothes again and shouted back, "You know, cleanliness is next to godliness." It was a threshold moment for Bey. He stepped back as if struck by lightning. Ione looked up and realized that Neah was having one of his come-to-Jesus moments. No bother, Ione was used to her husband's numerous quirks.

Now Bey understood how to attack this one problem from within. He smiled at Joyce, and she jiggled back. Bey walked back into the house and reached for the cookie jar, smiling. "So, Joyce flashed you with those store-bought knockers of hers?" Ione smiled wickedly. Neah was crushed. Store bought? He hung his head low in mock scorn and displeasure.

The appointed hour arrived. It was time for the traditional harvest celebration, held when the grapes had been picked, the silage turned one last time, the lofts packed full of dried fruit, and the root cellars packed with vegetables. The entire village gathered briefly in the town square, sang some folk tunes, and then happily filed into the church for an evening of tea and cider. The Germans had vacated the street and were holding some militaristic celebration at the school, now turned into a billet and armory. As the appointed hour arrived, some of the townsfolk who were not making the trip began to noisily drift away from the church. They entered the houses of friends and neighbors and turned on lights or lit candles in numerous windows.

Later, they planned to sneak back and extinguish those lights in an attempt to fool the Germans into thinking that nothing was amiss.

Those planning to leave had gathered in the basement to begin the final loading of clothing and food. The young priest had elected to stay in the sanctuary and play a few soft piano tunes to mask the noise of children and adults beginning their trek. He heard the rumble of the commandant's car entering the town square, even over the noise of the piano. No, his ear picked up another sound, a heavier sound. It was a tank following the commandant's car.

He kept playing but looked over his shoulder from time to time; surely those in the basement had heard and felt the approaching war machine. They must have already made their escape. They must have, he told himself again. The main sanctuary door opened and the commandant entered the church. He was alone. The German nodded to the priest as if to say, "Please continue playing." The young priest complied, slightly increasing the pace and volume of the tune. The commandant sat in the very first row behind the priest, and crossed his leg. His suspended foot kept time with the folk tune.

First one tune, and then another, and another; the priest played continuously. Sweat had long since soaked his garb and started to run off his hands, making the keys slick. Suddenly, the commandant pushed the priest to one side of the piano bench and said simply, "A duet?"

He began to play an old but familiar German farming tune. The priest joined in. They played quite well together. The tune ended. The commandant put his arm around the priest and said, "You play very well, my friend, very well indeed! That was fun!" He smiled broadly and increased the imprisoning strength of his grip around the younger man. "But I am afraid that we shall never play again together nearly as well, no, not nearly as well."

Two German soldiers who had entered the church seized the priest from behind and held his hands upon the ivory keys. "Now, priest, where are they?" The commandant's smile had gone away.

The priest stammered in fear, "I, I don't know what you mean." The commandant nodded and one of the soldiers took a pair of pruning shears and lopped off the little finger on the priest's left hand.

He screamed and writhed in agony. "No! No!" he shouted. Another finger left his hand. He screamed and kicked and blood spurted from his hand, across the piano keys. When the third finger was gone, he shouted, "The basement, in the basement!" He did not lapse into unconsciousness until after the machine guns had stopped.

———————

Bey was never allowed to do the wash in their house. Underwear, jeans, red shirts, black socks—did they really care who they rubbed up against in the washer? He had worked for the fire department for a while and not one of his fellow firedogs had ever asked a car crash victim or a heart attack sufferer if they had clean underwear on. He helped load the washer and handed Ione the soap. She used her proprietary method of scooping out a handful of soap and tossing that in the water. She leaned over and inspected the mix for a moment, and then took about two finger pinches worth more of soap and added that to the froth and churn. Ione always separated the whites from the colors and underwear from the towels.

Years ago when Ione was laid up after a bit of surgery and Bey was required to do the wash, Ione crawled out of bed, down the two sets of stairs from the bedroom to the laundry room, and watched every move Neah made. She did not offer simple advice in her weakened condition; instead, she gave sharp orders as to what she expected. Then he had to make her breakfast in bed and vacuum the front room, straighten the papers, clean the oven, and set out the fixings for dinner. Neah wondered why her being under the weather was likely going to kill him.

That night, after serving her dinner in bed as a special treat, Neah went to the laundry room and emptied the soap box into a Tupperware container and took the box out to the office. He read the ingredients and did a web search for the chemicals he knew nothing about. Security when doing a search is important, which is why the server Bey used was routed almost to the moon and back before it attached to the Smith House in Washington, D.C.

On the next trip to the store, Bey picked up several of the little travel-sized boxes of a variety of laundry soaps and fabric softeners. Ione wondered what he was up to and took the opportunity between aisles five and six at the local Safeway to remind him not to get any ideas about doing the laundry.

The store's night stocker was a chunky floozy with her head held together by a collection of pink curlers. "I had the same problem with my ex. Then I kilt him for ruining one of my lacy personal garments, things that need to be dry cleaned, you know, thongs and bustiers and stuff." Bey grimaced at an unpleasant mental image.

Ione turned to Bey and said, "See what can happen if you try to do the wash?"

The night stocker blew a pink bubble from an un-imaginably large wad of gum in her mouth and said, "You go, sister!"

Wide-eyed at the spectacle of a face obscured by a pink bubble haloed by pink curlers, Bey fled to the produce section to hide until Ione was finished shopping.

At home in the office, Bey ran some more searches for information on the contents of the soaps and softeners he had picked up. When he had compiled a list of general ingredients needed to formulate certain chemical compounds, he had it circuitously routed to Dr. Lucerne. Bey asked her to think about these chemicals for a bit. He was formulating other aspects of the plan.

Bey emailed the Smiths and asked them who did sales or public relations for the firm. One of the Mr. Smiths called him on a scrambler phone and asked why a clandestine organization would need a PR firm. Bey explained to him what it was he had on his mind and the resources he needed to make it happen. The Washington operator said he would get back to Bey in seventy-two hours with the answers.

In less than that time he was provided with a contact in Tacoma. Bey called and set a date. It was a pleasant drive to Tacoma. Traffic was light, and it was not raining. Bey was headed to one of the old warehouse buildings that had been nicely refurbished in the central business district. The contact, Molson Holden, was taller than Bey, but then most people were. He did not have the midnight mark, so Bey had to carefully steer the conversation.

Bey held out some sample copy and pictures of what

he would like to have the final product look like. There was a picture of the pope wearing the tall hat. He appeared to be waving in the general direction of the person who would be picking up the box. On the front side of the box, somewhere near the pope, was the quotation in Spanish as well as Portuguese: "Cleanliness is next to godliness!" On the proposed side panels the quotation was repeated in some of the major dialects used by the native populations of South America and Africa. Bey wanted the same general message conveyed on six different drafts. Even though the product in all the boxes would be the same, it was evident that the buying public sometimes preferred a product in a blue box to one in a pink box. Some of the pope shots were changed to happy mommy shots, or happy laundry worker shots. Molson took Bey's ideas and smiled politely. It was obvious he preferred to handle the creation of the artwork and such. Bey suggested another meeting in two weeks.

He then flew back to see Dr. Lucerne. Selah met him at the door and ushered him into the study. Dr. Lucerne rose and shook his hand. "Welcome back, and I made sure the weather was ferocious. Please don't fail to thank me for making your stay in the Northeast as miserable as possible." Indeed, the drive had been filled with some white-knuckle moments, caused not so much by the blowing snow and ice as by the kids sledding over the highway. The four-wheel drive Bey had picked up handled the road and climate well enough. And when the moose ran out into the road he was grateful for the antilock braking system. *Moose*, thought Bey; *who said God does not have a sense of humor?*

Bey gave Dr. Lucerne a copy of the list of the soap and softener chemicals. She said she would have to think about the exact mix. They chatted for two hours about the various conditions in which the product would be used. The climate was of particular interest for Dr. Lucerne. In hot and dry climates, people did not perspire the same as those in a humid climate. "Well, these little details will have to be worked out. People might get suspicious if all the women started growing beards and mustaches, and then men began developing breasts. Would serve you males right to have breasts and the entire hullabaloo associated with modified sweat glands."

Bey looked up from the data they were reviewing. "Modified sweat glands?"

Dr. Lucerne nodded.

"You really know how to cloud my little dreams and those of young men everywhere. I am saddened to think that the expression 'T and A' will be torn asunder and reconfigured as 'MSG and A'; it does not have the same impact."

Dr. Lucerne smiled at him. "You are a naughty little boy."

Well, she was right on that point, Bey smirked.

They spent the next day and a half working through details related to climates, local water conditions, and the formulas that could be used. At times Dr. Lucerne consulted some thick tome from her library and made shorthand notes on three-by-five cards. Bey offered her the use of his tablet; she declined, preferring to rely on her own tried-and-true method, which she had used for fifty-some years. Over the course of the time they were together, she used dozens of the cards, and filed them away in an ancient leather-bound recipe box. She pulled some colored tabs out of her desk and filed the cards in some special order behind them. Selah was kept busy running into the nearby village for supplies and food. Bey stayed at the local hotel. It was modest, yet comfy.

The Smiths had a special connection dropped into the study so Bey and Dr. Lucerne could access the internet and some other sources. Whatever they needed, it arrived shortly. Dr. Lucerne asked politely if being showered with supplies and information made Bey think he was superior. Bey thought for a moment and said, "No, not in the least, it is work that has to be done in a timely manner, and the organization does not like the staff sitting around playing cards or grab ass."

Selah knocked softly on the study door and slowly swung the door open. She was a stout woman who seemed to dote on the good doctor at all times. Out of the corner of his eye, Bey could see that her expression was changed. He turned and tuned in. Dr. Lucerne looked up and noticed the same thing. "Selah, what's wrong?"

Selah's face was a little ashen; however, she was still in control of herself. "There was a car and two men in the parking lot and on the road home." Her voice trailed off. Bey stood and went to his attaché.

Omak had selected two men from the list of names provided him through his computer: Tonasket, from the Ukraine, and a U.S. citizen named Pasco. Tonasket was going to be the leader of the two-man hit team. He had street cred from working with the Russian Mafia, both in Europe and in L.A. Brutal, unimaginative, but smart enough to handle two women and a government flunky named Bey. Pasco, on the other hand, was as dumb as a stump. His only saving graces were that he took orders well, did not question anything, and never interrupted a conversation. Omak looked over Pasco's rap sheet and glanced at him. Pasco was completely devoid of expression. Omak wondered if anything ever crossed his mind other than cheap liquor, cheap women, and hurting other people. For Pasco this was going to be a one-way trip. Tonasket and Omak had already decided that Pasco was not going to survive to cash in. After the hit, Tonasket was going to be whisked to JFK and loaded onto a plane that would take him to Heathrow for his next assignment, and to allow him to cool off before returning to North America.

Omak laid out the plan, showing the men the pictures he had taken, the available ground cover, how the house was laid out, and some very detailed satellite imagery. He had gone to the local building department and searched the public records for information on the house itself. Dr. Lucerne had at some point installed new plumbing and wiring. All the details of the floor plan were dutifully recorded. These he passed on to Tonasket. Pasco wouldn't understand them, anyway.

Using one of his aliases, Omak had rented a used car with all-wheel drive from an establishment that rented wrecks and asked few questions. He handed the keys over and told the men to hit the house around four that afternoon. He told them he was catching a flight to Phoenix and would read all about it in the morning newspapers. That was a lie. By the time the men arrived, walking to the house from opposite directions, Omak was forty yards away as well. He wore his camouflaged suit. He watched the scene play out, using his small binoculars.

Dr. Lucerne patted Selah on the arm and said, "Now, there is no reason for alarm. We have the advantage of a highly trained and competent observer here, and oh, yes, we have him, too." Bey turned to look at the doctor, and it appeared that she meant every word of what she had said. Dr. Lucerne asked Selah to leave and go to her quarters and prepare.

Bey was going to ask, "Prepare for what?" However, the situation warranted action, not questions and answers.

With Selah gone, Bey pulled out his slightly customized .45 automatic and tucked it into his waistband, and then placed four extra magazines into his pockets. Bey turned to go to the double French doors that led out into the rear yard and was startled to see Dr. Lucerne in possession of a sawed-off semiautomatic shotgun, a very nice Remington twelve gauge in three-inch magnum. She jacked a round into the chamber and replaced the chambered shell, dropping a new round into the tube with a practiced hand. "Uhhh, Doctor, I don't know what you are thinking, but I'd prefer that you and Selah stay in the house while I take a look around," Bey admonished.

Dr. Lucerne lowered the muzzle so that it pointed at Bey's midsection. "Look, Stuffy, I've been using blasters like this longer than you have been alive. So don't get pissy with me."

There was a pause in the conversation for a second or two. "Well, then, would you entertain the notion of watching this device and covering my ass while I take a walk?" He handed her a portable small flat screen TV that was hooked into a rooftop camera the Smiths had installed when they did the secured internet connection. She took the device and played with the pan and tilt control.

"What's that?" She was frowning at the handheld

screen. She turned it in Bey's direction. Something that looked like a rod was pointed at the house. But most rods do not have front sights and flash suppressors.

"Down!" Bey dove for the doctor and took her feet out from under her. The glass in the French door splintered into a thousand shards. Bey and the doctor went down in a heap behind the desk. Round after round thumped into the hardwood. Bey pulled the doctor towards him.

"Are you all right?" With one hand holding her behind the shoulder, he brushed the hair out of her face.

Her eyes focused on his face, finally. "You do this to impress all your favorite girls, or just old women in distress?" More rounds thumped into the desk. Glass sprinkled down on them.

"Where is the monitor?" Bey asked.

She felt around to her side, and brought up the display. She batted Bey's hand away and adjusted the pan and tilt. In a heartbeat, she had the muzzle centered in the screen. "I am very capable of taking care of myself, Stuffy." Bey concluded that mentioning that his name was not Stuffy could wait for later, if there was a later.

Bey looked over her shoulder and then glanced out over the top of the splintered desk. It took two glimpses to find the tree from where the shooter was blazing away. Bey began counting each shot softly under his breath, and watched for the muzzle to dip, indicating a reload process. There was a lull. The doctor stood up and grabbed the shotgun from the floor. "Son of a bitch!" She fired away. Bark flew off the tree. Bey brought up the heavy auto and aimed at an exposed calf muscle. There was a single crack of the pistol, and the snow was splattered with red. A grunt of pain could be heard all the way into the study.

They could hear the rear door being kicked in. The .45 spoke again, and there appeared to be more red on the snow. The muzzle of their assailant's gun swung around towards the house and barked again. Without so much as a flinch, Dr. Lucerne raised the Remington to her shoulder and fired. She scarcely winced with the recoil. The buckshot hit something. A dark figure was pushed away from the trunk of the maple by the force of the impact. Bey leveled the .45 against the doorjamb and shot twice towards the center of the dark shape. It collapsed onto the ground. Bey rapidly changed magazines, even though he had only fired a few times. Full magazines in the left pocket, partials in the right, empties get tossed, a mantra from long ago. Bey turned towards the study door and made sure the doctor was in a position of relative safety. She was busily slamming more shells into the tube.

Bey pushed the door open with his foot and glanced to the right and then to the left. The doctor was now camped out on his shoulder. "The rear door is open. That's the door into the kitchen. From there, they can go either into the living room, this way, or into Selah's quarters." Bey nodded and checked the floor in front of them. There were no footprints or piles of snow. Keeping low, he crab-walked to the kitchen entry. The rear door was hanging at a crazy angle from just the lower hinge. He could hear whimpering and the shuffle of feet. A voice boomed, "Come on out or the bitch eats it through the ear hole!" Bey froze, running through options. "I said come on out, and I meant now!" Selah screamed in pain. Bey stood up and entered the doorway of the kitchen. Selah was in the grasp of an armed man who was deliberately grinding the muzzle of a revolver into her ear.

"Let's take it easy now, we can work something out," said Bey, trying to sound reassuring. With his peripheral vision, he could see the doctor slowly slinking from the hall to his left into the front room. Bey wished she would act a little more like a damsel in distress; this could look bad on his annual evaluation. Bey moved a foot or so to the right, trying to shield the entry of the front room from the gunman's glances.

"Where is the doctor?" the gunman asked. He started to grind the muzzle into Selah's ear again. Selah wailed in pain and fear, although her eyes were fixed directly on Bey's.

"Your guy with the long gun shot her through the heart; she's in the study, dead. Very dead," Bey said.

The man looked from side to side with quick glances. "Where is Tonasket? Where is Tonasket now?"

Bey shrugged. "How should I know? He might be walking up behind you right now." Pasco turned, just a little, and the muzzle of the revolver came off Selah's ear and was pointed behind her into the space between them. Selah tilted her head away from Bey's line of fire. How did she know to do that? This was Bey's chance. He started to bring the automatic up, and the guy's right calf, the one closest to the front room, turned to mush.

The blast from a shotgun in close quarters is always a noisy affair. He turned; the doctor shouted, "Selah, down!" Selah collapsed to the floor. Bey had the pistol all the way up, and fired once, hitting the gunman just below the tip of his nose. The back of his head ballooned out and made a nasty mess on the wall behind him. With the medulla oblongata destroyed, there would not be even a jerk or a twitch. Very much like a rag doll, Pasco slumped down; unfortunately, he fell across the already traumatized Selah. She began to push the dead man off of herself unaided.

Bey motioned that the doctor should take Selah to the study, and view the exterior again through the camera. Bey made a quick check to verify that bad guy number one was deceased. He was. Exiting through the shattered remains of the rear door, Bey edged alongside the house until he was at the corner of the study and the side yard. A quick glance told him that bad guy number two was lying face up in the snow near the tree. The rifle was still in his grasp. Bey scuttled over to a stone monument and glanced towards the study.

The doctor leaned out and whispered, "I don't see anyone else, and Selah says there were only two in the car that followed her in town." Bey took a longer look at the prone form. No use in taking any chances; Bey shot the figure in the nearest foot. This did not elicit any sort of response, so Bey took a chance and figured that this gunman was just as dead as the man in the kitchen. He crouched, ran over, and leaned low against the tree. The prone figure was a man, shot in the leg, chest, neck, and more recently, the foot. Dr. Lucerne came up behind Bey and looked down at the still-warm corpse. Vapor wafted up from the vacant face. "Shooting him in the foot? Jesus, you got a real shitty bedside manner, Stuffy."

They went into the study. Bey used his scrambler to call the Smiths. It was late enough in the day that it would be dark soon; the light snowfall would mask the scene shortly. Bey asked if any of the shots could have been heard out on the road, or by neighbors. Dr. Lucerne said, "Look, Stuffy, this is Maine. We hunt here, we shoot here, and we blow things up here. No one will care or call." Selah was checking out the doctor for injuries at the same time the doctor was checking her out. She stiffened when the doctor placed a cold compress against her ear.

Selah asked calmly, "Who were they?" A fair question. Bey searched the stiff in the kitchen. Wallet, pocketknife, a knife in a sheath at the ankle, a small revolver in a back pocket. A cheap watch, clothes off the rack, and leather-soled shoes to walk in the snow. Somewhat unprofessional. The other guy was clearly the brains of the operation, as he carried the car rental form and an airline ticket for one person. So, the guy in the kitchen was not expected to go home, regardless of the outcome, or he was a local. Bey didn't think that typical Maine residents would have prison tattoos and tattoos of gang characters on their forearms, and what appeared to be old burns of some sort around the nostrils and the corners of the mouth. The rental car yielded little in the way of additional information.

Bey tidied up the kitchen and temporarily rehung the back door. Dr. Lucerne told him where to find some thin plywood and a cordless screw gun, so he was able to board over the windows in the study.

It took them five hours to arrive, they got to the house around two in the morning. They were the Smith family cleanup crew. They politely shoved Bey, Selah, and the doctor into the front room and kept them there while they scrubbed and cleaned and took pictures, sketches, and statements. Bey would get a complete report in a few days; he was forced to promise to share it with the doctor. While they waited, Bey and the doctor contin-ued to flesh out the rest of the program and attempted to ease Selah's discomfort, real or imagined, by plying her with some Baileys Irish Cream. At least, that was the idea in Bey's heart.

The Smiths left a vial of pills for Selah, which she ig-nored. Bey began to formulate the idea that Selah was more than just a simple Maine housekeeper. The Smiths were gone by nine in the morning, and Bey followed them out the door, after having them check his rental for explo-sives. Bey clenched his teeth just a little when he cranked the engine over.

There is a sense of humor in the gray government busi-ness: one of the Smiths had set the radio to the loudest rock station he could find. The crew also adjusted the vol-ume to somewhere above "stun." When the engine fired and Bey thought he had cheated death, the radio kicked on, scaring him enough to make him jump. He slammed the steering wheel with his hand. "You guys are bastards!" he shouted.

The OnStar kicked on, and a small voice said, "Oh, no, we're not!" Bey gave the speaker a clearly understood ges-ture with his hand. The voice said, "That is just plain rude."

With that, the radio switched over to some off-the-wall southern religious station that appealed to snake han-dlers. Bey was unable to change the channel or reduce the volume for the entire drive to the airport.

Omak froze against the ground when he caught sight of a minuscule motion on the roof of Lucerne's house. In the foreground he could see Tonasket blazing away with the machine gun. To his right, he saw Pasco begin kicking in the kitchen door. Yet by happenstance, he saw the shadow of a movement on the roof. His initial thought—that Lucerne and Bey perished in the first volley—vanished. Someone was controlling the camera on the roof. He wanted to shout a warning to his goons, but then thought to himself, *"It's what they are paid to do. Let's see how this turns out."* In moments, Tonasket was down. Pasco was out of sight in the house. From the direction of the shattered remains of the kitchen door, he thought he could hear shouting, but with Tonasket's hammering with the machine gun, it was he wasn't sure if the shouting was figment or actuality.

Muzzle flashes backlit the kitchen curtains. He could see silhouettes moving against them. He saw Bey slide through the kitchen door, creep around the corner of the house, and do everything by the book. Head bobbing, eyes moving, ears seeking. Although being in a room where there had been gunfire made the use of his ears suspect. This distinctive behavior made Omak change his entire attitude towards and perception of Bey. This was no mere government flunky; this was not a desk jockey from some mundane division of the Department of Health and Human Services. Bey was trained; Bey was *experienced.* Omak inscribed a note in his guts to never underestimate Bey again. Within a few minutes, Lucerne and Bey had sifted through Tonasket's pockets and returned to the house. Omak lay there for some time, until the darkness gathered. He was an actor awaiting his cue. There! The camera began to slowly and methodically scan from a point just to the left of dead Tonasket. It acted like Bey's head, moving, bobbing, and weaving. From time to time it froze and held for a moment before moving on. Omak rose up on an elbow and studied the camera and looked for the reasons why it froze. His heart skipped a beat. A family of raccoons scavenged in the fading light. The camera had thermal imaging.

In spite of his camouflaged suit, Omak was going to read like a volcano in an ice field when the camera completed its swing around the house. He rose and walked purposefully through the forest. In minutes, the subzero temperatures would cool the earth where he had lain. The darkness and the forest shielded him, and as the last rays of light were absorbed by the overcast dusk, Omak became one with the forest, a Wendigo and nothing more.

Neah Bey had a cup of coffee with Ione at the kitchen table on a dreary Saturday morning. Since Neah and Ione were getting started a little later than usual, the cats were intent on getting a greater measure of affection from them. Euripides the Wonder Cat jumped on the table and carefully inspected each item that he found there. Satisfied, he plopped down and extended a large mitten over to Ione's arm.

Euripides stared at Neah until his chin sank down to the tabletop and his eyes closed. Neah took the cat's snoring as a message that it was time for him to shower and start more of his paperwork. He had a videoconference with the Smiths later.

He adjusted the temperature to be just below scalding and enjoyed the water beating into his muscles. Years before, Ione had given him a fog-free mirror that he used for shaving while in the shower. Neah had suggested that he put in a heated towel rack adjacent to the shower, but Ione said that seemed a little frivolous. He stepped out onto the shower mat and made a quick wipe across the larger bathroom mirror. The toothbrush rested in a small glass jar that had formerly been a container for some of Ione's tea. Neah picked up the toothbrush and applied a dab of toothpaste. He centered his reflection in the cleaned area of the foggy mirror, and as the brush touched his lips, he stopped. He stared at his haloed image in the mirror, toothbrush just to the side of his lip.

Neah set the toothbrush back in the jar. His fingers traced over every over-the-counter commodity on the tiled vanity top. Hand lotion. Body lotion. Aftershave. Toothpaste. Deodorant. Shampoo. Conditioner. Vitamins. Mineral supplements.

He opened the medicine cabinet that was off to one side. Here were a few of his prescriptions, including pills for his cholesterol and acid reflux, as well as an anti-inflammatory and a smattering of Ione's medications.

Neah closed the medicine cabinet and stared back into his fog-framed reflection. He smiled just a little, as one would imagine a spider would when the web trembles with fresh prey.

A few days later, Bey received a forwarded email from Dr. Lucerne. She had come up with several formulas for him that could work in wide geographical areas. There was a note: "Women will not grow facial hair, or become muscle-bound nincompoops like men. Men will remain as stupid and uncaring as before; they will not grow breasts or want to see a greater number of chick flicks." Sadly, Dr.

Lucerne had by accident or intent copied the Smiths on the email.

As expected, one of the Smiths called Bey and wondered just what he was up to.

Bey flew to Los Angeles with Ione. They stayed out in Orange County at a nice hotel made out of an old lentil silo. They had been there before and had enjoyed the place, and its easy access to the freeways. They drove down through Laguna Canyon, then up the coast to Long Beach. They dined in L.A., then went back to the hotel for a pleasant evening of reading. If the events of the last few days had made an impact on Bey, he did not allow it to alter his exterior. Inside, he was being torn apart in many directions. He considered his affection for his wife and his desire to be with her, and his desire to protect Dr. Lucerne and Selah. He checked his phone so often that Ione asked if he were seeing other women. He said, "Well, at least two others." They had a good laugh about that.

The next day, Bey dropped Ione off at the huge nearby mall and went on to a meeting with one of the larger soap manufacturers on the West Coast. Individual companies make certain soap products to sell as prized name-brand items, using special ingredients. However, most soap products are produced in bulk and then shipped and packaged nearer the end user. The plant sales manager, Pomeroy Gorst, handed Bey some small boxes of product, and then a hard hat and safety glasses. The two men walked all over the plant and watched machines grind, sift, and containerize tons of soap. Gorst was a bundle of excitement and enthusiasm about his product. Bey was polite even after he discovered that Gorst's most beloved soap made his eyes water and was irritating the inside of his nose.

In the end, Bey placed an order for five hundred thousand pounds of the soap, with the proviso that it had to be specially processed. Pomeroy wanted to know exactly how specially. The chemicals that Dr. Lucerne required were found in a dry powder form, so all the manufacturer needed to do was to simply empty fifty-gallon drums of stuff into the last mixer in the plant.

"What material are we talking about here?" Pomeroy asked.

Bey patted him on the shoulder and said, "If I told you, I'd have to kill you."

Pomeroy laughed.

Bey laughed. Bey then said, "Well, we have done a lot of research into the climates and the conditions of the places the product will be used, and we consider our addition a proprietary substance that makes your already fine product work better. We'll be basically giving the soap away for the first year of the program and measuring its success, and all future orders for similar amounts will be conditioned on the results."

Pomeroy brightened up. "If there are other orders of this size on a regular basis, we might be able to study the cost per pound issue even more closely." They shook hands at the plant office where Bey handed in his hard hat and safety glasses. Pomeroy stopped smiling for a minute. "Please realize that I will have to ask what the substance is that you will be adding to our product." Bey told him that a complete breakdown of the adjuncts would be faxed to him in the next few days, along with a material safety data sheet.

Pomeroy's insistance on having the ingredients identified meant that Bey had to create another step in the production process. The chemicals that Dr. Lucerne required to be in the mix would have to be shipped to a distant warehouse. In the warehouse, those chemicals would be repackaged and placed in new containers with reasonably accurate labels, then shipped again, to Stellar Soap Products of Orange County, California, as innocuous soap additives.

When Bey got to the car, he used his scrambler phone and outlined the new wrinkle in the process to a Miss Smith.

This Miss Smith sounded quite young, possibly barely old enough to work. Over time, Bey had seen a large spread in the ages of workers in the foyer of Smith, LLC. This Miss Smith sounded professional and direct. She repeated back to him the details, and ended the conversation with, "Unless you are notified otherwise, your original chemicals will be shipped from Stamford, Connecticut, to a Smith, LLC warehouse in East St. Louis. The repack will take place there. The new shipment will carry the labeling we discussed and will ship to the Stellar Soap Products of Orange County. Correct?" Bey agreed, and the call was over.

He then followed up with the Tacoma package designer. When Bey called, Molson Holden was on the phone with someone else, but he called Bey back within ten minutes, as his receptionist had promised. "Hello, I thought you might be calling; here is what we have done. The covers are finished, the side panels are finished, and the directions for use are completed. We can send via fax or we can mail or hand-deliver copies of the artwork to you." Bey told him to start faxing and he would get them on his wireless computer. They came through, and they looked even better than Bey could have hoped for.

Bey picked up Ione, and she insisted that he tour part of the mall with her. It was a grand place, and there were more than enough stores to wander through. They drove over to Huntington Beach and ate at a nice restaurant overlooking the ocean.

The next day, they loafed around, hitting a few small shops and a bookstore before heading to the airport. Bey checked in with the home office and told a Miss Smith to confirm their flight time and to check to see whether there were any security issues that might delay their return to Seattle. They enjoyed watching the setting sun over the Pacific Ocean, looking out of the left side of the plane on the way north.

Bey drove down to Tacoma on Monday and finalized the artwork with Molson Holden. Holden would find a box company and order the boxes. Stellar Soap would use one of their machines to ready the boxes, another to drop the treated soap into them, then another to hot glue the tops. For an additional cost, Stellar would palletize the boxes, then shrink-wrap the pallets and load them onto a Smith, LLC semitrailer.

Smith, LLC would then drive the trailer to El Paso, where the load would be broken down and disbursed to a variety of shippers. It's all about giving people choices, Bey had explained to the Smiths.

The buying power of Smith, LLC made it able to sell soap in two dozen countries cheaper than the locals could manufacture it. Of course, Smith, LLC was receiving some clandestine subsidies, which is one of the benefits of being gray. Smith, LLC and a number of other fictitious companies donated tons of soap to the UN, UNESCO, the Red Cross and Red Crescent, and dozens of local charities and relief agencies. Bey marked April 2 as the kickoff date for Smith, LLC's new product.

Bey flew back to see Dr. Lucerne. Phase two was coming up, and he needed her input on that part, too. Selah opened the door and scowled at him.

"No trouble this time, eh?"

Bey nodded and stepped forward.

Selah put her hand on his chest. "No trouble this time, or you don't come in, eh?"

Thwarted from entering without making a fuss, Bey put his arms around Selah and gave her a hug. "No trouble this time, baby."

She smiled broadly and let him in. It was a promise he could make; there had been rotating teams of Smith agents trailing, leading, dogging, and encircling Dr. Lucerne and Selah since the awful day of carnage on Bey's last visit. The Smiths provided an envelope of protection that could not be seen or heard—it was like a veil of gray in the fog. Sensors, cameras, and other detectors had been installed on the phone, in the house, in and on the house and the three outbuildings, and in the surrounding woodlands. From what the lead Smith agent told him when he checked in with him at Portland's airport, they had enough video of deer and moose and squirrels to make Marlin Perkins jealous. Good; Bey had no desire to be a liar, or get shot at again, or see the doctor or Selah come to harm.

The doctor was in her study. The bulletproofing in the French door was not all that noticeable. A thicker, more industrial-strength framing had replaced the former look of the door and the adjacent windows. Good. Dr. Lucerne was too valuable a commodity to put at risk. Bey understood that she had put up a fuss for a bit, and he fully expected to be browbeaten over the modifications.

"Hello, Stuffy! How are you today?" She gave him a good handshake and sat back down. She waved him towards a love seat set off to the side of the fire. "What have you got this time for me to ponder?" She seemed cheerful enough; maybe the first touches of spring had lightened her spirits. Birds chirped, and the buds were clearly evident on the trees and shrubs.

Bey took out a manila folder holding eight-by-ten color photographic prints. Bey and others had taken these photos. They were pictures of large and small crowds of people going about their lives, in barrios and small villages, at school assemblies, and in town meetings, from high in the Andes to the Caribbean, to the Amazon, to Central and West Africa, to parts of the Middle East and the Indian subcontinent. There were pictures of village elders sitting around a small fire, and of children, young adults, and couples, of all ages, colors, shapes, and manner of dress. There were sixty-five pictures in all. The doctor looked at each one. A couple of times, she took out a lighted magnifying glass and studied something that she fancied.

"Well, other than you took a lot of pictures, what the hell is this supposed to mean?" she asked. Bey was slightly energized and at the same time relieved that he did not have her as a professor in some college class. She set the pictures down. Bey sat still for a moment. She had to see it herself, and she needed to find it alone.

"Look again," Bey said.

"What the hell for?" She frowned, unaccustomed to being told what to do.

He sighed. "Look again, *please.*"

She frowned again and took up the pictures and the magnifying glass. She went over every inch of the pictures, face by face, locale by locale. On the side, she used an old fountain pen to make cryptic notes on her stack of three-by-five cards. An hour passed. Selah was called in to prepare a cup of tea and some cookies.

Finally, Dr. Lucerne set the pictures down and examined her notes. From the center drawer of her desk, she withdrew a small calculator. She reviewed her notes, and made calculations. About a half hour passed. "Okay, Stuffy, here are the facts. I have surmised that forty-five percent of these pictures came from the Western Hemisphere, or the New World, whichever you prefer; I hope this doesn't confuse you. Fifty-five percent come from north of the equator. The equator is an imaginary line dividing the world around the middle. Someday you should go look for the line. I hear it's lovely in the springtime. Sixty-five percent of the identifiable people are women. Seventy-five percent of all the women are of childbearing years, although that percentage might be conditional on overall health and other local issues. Sixty-five percent again are of dark-skinned races, being native, Spanish, African, or Asian, or mixes thereof. There are signs of electrical power in about half the pictures. Running water appears to be nonexistent in almost all of the pictures. There are accumulations of litter and trash in almost all pictures. There appears to me to be open sewers in five of the pictures." She sat back and took a sip of tea. Bey dreaded telling her to look again. "Oh, yeah, and Stuffy? Someone is making a killing selling tee shirts of sports and rock stars all over the world." Bingo.

Bey reached into his case and pulled out a tee shirt

from Gennera Sportswear, formerly of Seattle. They had a product that changed colors on the wearer depending upon body heat. "Here, look at this." He laid the shirt on her desk.

"Gee thanks, pick this out for me all by yourself?" She held the shirt up and examined it briefly. "I suppose this is your choice of after dinner wear at Hooters?"

Man, Bey thought, *she is a tough nut.*

"Is this something you want me to model in a wet tee shirt contest?" she continued. Bey did his best to refrain from smiling.

"Actually, Doctor, if you lay the shirt on the desk and place your palm on it for a few seconds, I think you'll get the point of this exercise." Bey got a "Harrumph!" for his efforts, but she did as she was asked.

She removed her hand, however, her palm and finger patterns remained. "And this excites you how? Oh, I get it; with this, wet tee shirt night is just sooooo much better." Bey took out an article from a Japanese newspaper that had been translated into English. There was a photo of the inventor and his models wearing normal looking articles of clothing. The article described how the clothes could be impregnated with vitamins, minerals, drugs, medicines, and other additives that could be absorbed through the skin. Certain individuals lack the ability to absorb various vitamins, minerals, and the like through their digestive tracts. The wearer needed only to put on his or her special undershirt tank top to get a measured dose of vitamin C all day long.

The doctor read the article over at least twice, then looked at the thermal tee shirt in front of her, and then at the stack of pictures. "Stuffy, I must confess that your thought processes just don't go down the same path as everybody else's, do they?"

Bey had been told that before, but people will tell you anything when you are holding a gun to their head. "Thank you, Doctor; I take that as a compliment."

She looked up from her notes. "Don't. It's like someone telling you that you have the best case of Ebola they have ever seen."

Darn, Bey thought, *I'm just never going to get an ounce of slack here.*

They pulled out the tomes they had looked at before and began laying out a program. Dr. Lucerne would work on the chemicals and drugs, like before. Bey asked for several circumstances to be addressed. She agreed with his concerns and assessments and added a few of her own.

The Smiths had requested that Bey visit them in D.C. They had a car waiting for him at Dulles airport. In the backseat of the limo was a small folder that the driver told Bey he should study on the way to the house. It was a cost breakdown of his activities to date. Included was a study of the projected benefits and impacts on the populations in question. According to the bean counters, everything was on track.

They pulled in through the gate, and Bey noticed a stern-looking man of about fifty dressed in a thick coat. You did not have to have the wits of much more than a department store elevator operator to figure out that he was an armed guard. He was wearing a radio earpiece with a coil that ran down the back of his neck and then disappeared under his coat. Bey decided to name him Tex.

"A welcoming committee just for me?" The driver looked over his shoulder at Bey and was not smiling. He pulled up in front of the door. Bey waited for the guard to open the door for him. *A-ha, not the case.* He got out and refrained from asking if he should tip or not. Bey took one step towards the house. Tex motioned for him to stop. Bey stopped. Tex looked over the compound, and chatted with someone on the radio. Tex then motioned for the car to leave. The gate stayed closed until the car stopped in front of it and waited for it to open. Tex communicated again with someone, and the gate opened. Across the street was a modest-sized delivery van with some unique features, including radio antennas, a small sat dish, and gun ports. Not your average delivery van.

The car left and the gate closed. Bey stood very still. The cameras were constantly in motion, and from slow glances to the left and right, Bey guessed that about fifty percent of the time they were pointing at him. Bey was beginning to hope that the low bidder did not install the system, and that the Smiths did not have a basement filled with minimum wagers manning the guns today.

Tex stepped towards Bey and squinted at his face; Bey got the cue and opened his eyes wide. He squinted slightly in the bright sunshine. "Okay, palm and a squint if you don't mind." Tex pointed with his chin at the retina scanning camera and palm reader located adjacent to the door. With the Smiths, it was all about redundancy. Bey did not mind at all, as now all the miniguns were pointed at him; he dutifully placed his palm on the reader and squared his face over the lens that would examine his eyes.

The door clicked, and Bey entered the reception area. A new Miss Smith sat at the reception desk. Her smile might just as well have been glued on. Bey moved slowly across the floor. "Hello, Miss Smith, I believe I have an appointment?" Bey was already sweating. She smiled, and a door clicked off to his left this time. A new door for Bey; it was the fifth and final one. It did not make him feel better.

The room behind the door was appointed like the other ones: it was sterile, with a single desk and a nameplate— "Mrs. Smith" this time. Mrs. Smith was on the phone and looking down through the glass top of her desk. Under the thick plate was an angled monitor. She waved him to the chair. "Thank you." Mrs. Smith hung up the phone.

"That was about Dr. Lucerne. She has sent in some formulas and other information that will be downloaded to your tablet before you leave." Mrs. Smith pecked at the desktop; there was a small emitter that created a virtual keyboard for her on the glass. "You have been busy. Very busy. We note that you have been very effective. And courageous, if what the doctor and the clean team have reported is true."

Oh, gosh, stop it please, Bey thought to himself. Bey sat. She sat.

"We like that in a, hmmm, employee?" She again pecked at the image of a keyboard. "Things are operating under a little bit of stress around here. Someone threw a satchel over the fence a few days ago and blew a hole in the geranium bed. Excluding the geraniums, no real harm. As you have noted, we have increased some security measures." She sat back in her chair.

"Well, here we are," she continued. Bey was beginning to get just a little edgy about this whole meeting thing. "The purpose of our little chat today is to hand this to you and make you aware of the problem." Out of the desk drawer, which she unlocked, she retrieved one of the hundreds of millions of manila folders that must exist in Washington,

D.C. In it there were some printed pages, and some pictures. The pictures sent Bey's blood into a boil in half a heartbeat. Here was a picture of Ione taken through the gun sight of a sniper rifle, the crosshairs resting on the bridge of her nose. Some of the pictures were of Bey at the soap factory, with the crosshairs on his heart. Others were of Ione and Neah shopping, holding hands, kissing goodbye in the morning, all with crosshairs lined up on heart, head, or neck.

Bey read the pages twice, having to take a few deep breaths in between. The text was a translation of a note that had been handwritten in Latin. The original note was in a plastic evidence bag.

"Those who trespass in God's work shall perish."

Bey set the folder down on the desk. "And?"

Mrs. Smith smiled back at him. "They told me you were a tough nut, or a nut case. Which is it?"

"Neither. I'm just mad," Bey said through clenched teeth, staring at the folder.

"Yes," she whispered, "I can understand that. Rest assured that we are covering Ione around the clock. Your neighbors were offered amounts they could not refuse for their houses to the north and south of you. We have checked out Joyce across the alley. She's clean, fake boobs and all."

Damn, Bey thought. *Does everyone know about my neighbor's breasts?*

"Your wife is not aware of the problem, and she is certainly not aware of the protection being afforded her." Mrs. Smith took another small folder from her desk and handed it to Bey. More good news? He took the folder and opened it. It contained a travel document with details of a trip on a chartered jet to a small island in the Caribbean, a check in the mid six digits, and necessary visas and the like. The jet would take off from Boeing Field in fourteen hours.

"We'll take care of you and your wife on the island until this cools down. When you return, your house will be painted and certain features will have been added. Tell your wife it's a company benefit. You'll be on ice for two weeks, but you will be working on the project in whatever free time you have. When you get back, you'll have new neighbors and two new cars. Nice, huh?"

Bey tapped the folder with the pictures of Ione being lined up for a kill shot. "Not really."

She frowned and nodded her head. "Yes. I suppose that it will be a race to see who gets to the shooter first, and then gets to extract the information he or she is carrying. Us or you."

Bey heard the door click, indicating that this conversation was over. Bey stands, she remains sitting. "They'll beg it's you and not me," he said, thinking, *schoolyard bullies make threats; professionals make and keep commitments.*

When the door closed behind Bey, Mrs. Smith slumped into the chair, her hand sliding off the pistol held in a bracket under the desk. Rumor had it that while Bey and his wife were on vacation a few years ago, a street thug had grabbed for Ione's purse. Bey had pushed the man away and scurried along the promenade with Ione. Rumor also had it that while his wife was sleeping that night, Bey left the hotel room and hunted the man down. What was not a rumor was that the next day a man was found choked to death in an alley after suffering substantial internal injuries.

Outside, Tex was waiting for him. He radioed for the

car, and the gate opened. This time he opened the door for Bey. As Bey got in, Tex whispered, "You can worry all you want, but no one is going to get past my people and get to your wife, ever." That made Bey feel a little better.

He was driven to a small government airfield on the north side of D.C. where a Gulfstream was wound up and waiting for him.

Bey was the only passenger. The door to the cockpit was substantial and locked. Service was excellent. He just had to wander around an empty plane and open cupboards and fridge units to find bags of nuts and bottled water by himself.

The Smiths had an armored Suburban waiting for Bey at the airport. Three tri-athlete-looking guys met his plane and shuffled him from the plane to the 'Burb. Not many people get to leave an airplane on the taxiway and get picked up basically by an armored personnel carrier. The radios squawked inside. The gentleman to Bey's right handed him a small notepad that had a map of Bey's house on it. It detailed the security measures that were in place, and those that would be installed when the Beys were gone.

Bey asked if any progress had been made on determining who had made the threats. The black man in the passenger seat turned around, his dreadlocks cascading over his shoulders. "Sorry, that would be a negative. We are still trying to find out what is going on. I will state, sir, in all candor, that you have more enemies than anybody else we have worked with."

Great; that ought to help narrow the search. Bey sighed.

Ione was up, tidying something in the kitchen. Bey always called before arriving at home, and did so this time.

It was a matter of courtesy, and Bey could read a great deal into his wife's voice. Advance knowledge would give him an edge if she were held under duress. They hugged a little longer than usual and kissed a little more passionately, in spite of being in front of the security detail.

The tallest of the three Smiths spoke up, which caught Bey off guard. "Ione? May I call you that?"

Ione, ever polite, said, "Yes?" She looked from person to person and stared questioningly at Bey.

"Thank you. As you know, your husband has been working on a lot of projects for the company. And, he may suspect, but most likely does not know, that we have selected him to take a two-week, all-expenses-paid vacation to a private island in the Caribbean. You will be waited on hand and foot. There has been a schedule set up that is most flexible, but generally consists of massages, spa treatments, and several unique tours of the island."

Ione looked a little stunned. "Well, honey, that's wonderful! I knew you were up to something important. Isn't this great?" Bey smiled in a halfhearted manner; he was wondering how he was going to get Ione onto a plane tomorrow morning at eight in the morning.

"In order to show the company's indebtedness to your husband, and to you and your support of him, we have chartered a flight leaving Boeing Field tomorrow morning at eight!"

Ione deflated a little. "So soon? I have to shop for clothes and pack!"

"You are absolutely right! And we have taken that into consideration as well. The charter jet will land at Miami International, and you will have ten hours of layover time to shop, all expenses paid, for anything you might need. Other items can be picked up on the island! Are you ready to have a good time? Are you ready to have a good time for free?"

This guy is a pro, thought Bey.

All three guys began shaking Bey's hand and clapping. Ione was overwhelmed. So was Bey.

Bey walked out to the car with them. "Jesus, you guys are pretty slick."

Tall Guy put his hand on Bey's shoulder. "Yeah, but for you and your wife, it just seems fair. I wonder what the Smiths will say about the shopping spree I threw in to help smooth things over." He shrugged, "Oh, well, would not be the first time I had to explain things in a new and different manner to avoid getting fired." They left.

They came back at 7:15 the next morning, and they introduced the cat sitter, a towering mountain of a human from whom the cats fled. From there the first stop they made, unasked, was the espresso shop at the Metro Market on Admiral Way. Bey bought a round of drinks for everyone. The Suburban easily handled the two small suitcases the Beys had been able to gather for the trip. Ione seemed to be looking forward to shopping. Miami was noted for having a classy concourse, and Ione remembered a Swarovski crystal shop from her last visit. Tall Guy blanched a little when Ione chatted about the wonderful crystal that could be found there.

It was a wonderful two weeks. Dr. Lucerne was a guest in a nearby bungalow, and she and Bey managed to monitor the soap production and distribution as well as work on the tee shirt issue.

When they returned back home, Ione noticed that windows were different, and there were other changes as well. Bey blew it off. "The company is upgrading security for all the senior staff. I told them to fix what they wanted while we were on vacation." Bey's explanation seemed to work. Over the years, Ione had become as adept as Bey at pointing out closed-circuit TV equipment, listening devices, beam detectors, security guards, and more. She did not seem to be too unhappy with everything. She waved across the alley at Joyce. Bey did not even bother to look up. He whispered to himself, "Store bought, woman, have you no shame?"

Omak sat in the hotel room and stared at the monitor. The message was simple, "Continue with plan." He took a towel and placed it over the monitor and then took a small battery-powered radio and sat it under the towel. Rock music filled the air. He pulled out his only real possession, the dog-eared and tattered envelope. Omak clutched it to his chest and began to softly weep. Tears stung his face as he pulled out his last picture of Roslyn and Lacey. They had been feeding birds along the shore of Lake Michigan in the early summer. He rocked back and forth a little, as if still holding Lacey in his arms to comfort her after she had been awakened by a bad dream. "Soon," he said, and rocked a little more, "soon."

Bey took to wearing a small commlink. Ione asked what it was, and he told her it was like a cellular phone. He did not elaborate on the fact that he used it to listen in to the security doings going on around them.

Ione made two "welcome to the neighborhood" baskets of cookies and quilted placemats. Then, somewhat uncharacteristically, she invited both sets of new neighbors and Joyce to an impromptu cocktail hour the next afternoon. The commlink buzzed until after eleven that evening, when Bey finally threw the damn thing in a drawer. Ione's invitation had screwed up the security coverage by forcing everyone who was pretending to be a neighbor to actually act like one. The security detail needed to call in extras to come in and man the parapets, as it were.

Bey stayed around Seattle for two weeks, generally trying to stay out from underfoot. Dr. Lucerne and Bey communicated often, sometimes several times a day, as they worked on the tee shirt project. Bey sent the Smiths out to get as many endorsements and permissions to use the likenesses of various rock stars, bands, sports figures, and others for the shirts as they could. They were very skilled in weaving a fine line between the United Nations, the NBA, the Red Cross, the NFL, MLB, and NASCAR.

In the meantime, in order to get a test market going, Smith, LLC was gleaning in every Goodwill, St. Vincent de Paul, and Salvation Army store in the United States. They were buying up every useable tee shirt that had someone, heck, anyone, on it. They were going to test the worldwide delivery system for the clothes of the future.

Ione asked him what he was doing, and in a roundabout way he told her the company was working on a charitable endeavor to get inexpensive clothing to those people in places that needed it most. "Do you suppose they clean the donated clothing before it goes overseas?"

Bey told her he would look into it. He kicked himself for missing the obvious chance to further speed the entire process. He dashed out to the office and got Dr. Lucerne and the Smiths into a special chat room. By the end of the following month, a national laundry service with facilities in every state would wash all the collected clothes for free, in a very special soap, and soak them in a very special sanitizing bath.

At the end of the chat, Mr. Smith wrote, "Good idea on the donated clothes. We are following up with other clothing providers around the world."

Bey typed in the true nature and source of the idea.

"Extend thanks to your wife. Your pay will be cut accordingly."

The Smiths logged out.

Dr. Lucerne fired a parting shot. "You dumb shit."

Bey grimaced.

It was time for Bey to go see Dr. Lucerne again. He got up around 2:30 in the morning and packed his small travel case. Absentmindedly, he put the commlink in his ear. It was silent. The hairs stood up on the back of his neck. There were hushed words spoken quickly.

"Target One, backyard of Joyce's. Silencer on small handgun." The link clicked.

"Target Two, dark blue sedan, four-door, two houses north, west side of road, using night vision equipment."

"Targets Three and Four, sitting in pickup truck three houses to the south, using radios."

Sweat started to drip down the back of Bey's neck. He

grabbed an old dark shirt and tucked the .45 into the elastic waistband of his boxers; they sagged dangerously low. Bey laid the gun down and slipped on a pair of Carhartt shorts with cargo pockets and a web belt. The automatic rode much better.

Omak had the world scanned for this mysterious Neah Bey. It took months of digging; thousands of feet of security tape were analyzed. Finally, an operative from the Pacific Northwest left a message in a secure blog. The blog had been set up at Omak's request, so that he could get a first read on incoming data from around the world. Most of what showed up there was religious drivel of those offering prayers, sacrifices, penance, and their lives. Occasionally, a bit of information piqued Omak's interest. Logging on, he'd encourage the writer to explore further. Most of the time, that was the end of it. This time, the writer attached a blurry cell phone picture of Neah Bey and some attractive woman at a grocery store coffee bar. The picture caused Omak to redden. It reminded him of simply enjoying the company of a loved one while doing something as trivial as having an espresso drink in public, something that he and Roslyn had done many times over the years. And yet, here was Bey, with a woman he obviously cared about, holding her hand in public, staring into her eyes. He closed the link and thought for many moments, and then reopened the blog. He arranged to communicate with the writer through a special secure chat room. It took a considerable amount of time to set up, owing to the extreme security measures employed.

<pre>
OMAK: Where was this picture taken?
WRITER: Grocery store.
OMAK: Which grocery store?
WRITER: The one at Admiral and 42nd in West Seattle.
OMAK: How long ago was the picture taken?
WRITER: Yesterday afternoon, they come here every
           now and then.
OMAK: Do you know who they are?
WRITER: No, they live near here.
OMAK: Can you find out where?
WRITER: I think so. Is this important?
OMAK: Only a little important.
WRITER: Did they do something wrong? Do you
           want me to say or do something?
OMAK: No. They might not be the right people. Find
           out where they live. No hurry. We are check-
           ing other people in San Diego, Milwaukee,
           and Cleveland to see if they are the ones we
           need to contact about an adopted relative.
           Please be discreet. No hurry. Thanks.
</pre>

Omak logged off. He disliked using unknown civilians to do his work. He hoped that Writer would do as he suggested and just find the address and not do anything blatant or just plain stupid.

In a few days, a special icon appeared on Omak's monitor. It had taken some effort to convince the person at the other end of the computer to stand watch over the blog and notify him the instant that Writer checked back in. Omak logged on. Writer had sent in an address and a picture that she, somewhat unwisely, had taken of the Bey's house. Writer provided the caption "In West Seattle."

Writer followed up by asking if there was anything she

should do to help—ask questions, introduce herself, or any of ten other things that would only serve to announce to Neah Bey, agent of the gray government, that he had been found at home. Omak thanked Writer and told her the rightful family had been found living in the Midwest, and the message about the adopted relative had been taken care of. "Thank you very much," typed Omak, "but please don't make contact as doing so might alarm an innocent family and cause them concern." Writer acknowledged that silence was for the best and asked again if there was anything else she could do to help. Omak responded that Writer had been a tremendous help, that he was appreciative of Writer's efforts, and that should the need arise he would get in touch with Writer again. Omak ended with "Please check back in about two weeks."

Omak stared at the transcript and muttered to himself, "The last person on this planet that is innocent is Neah Bey." The picture and address were used to further identify the Beys' house, the surrounding houses, the street layout, and the alleyway. Using considerable resources from the unlimited databases the Church maintained, Omak built a profile on the Beys and their neighbors. After much scrutiny, he determined that the neighbors were indeed just neighbors. It did not appear that there was much, if any, interaction between the Beys and their neighbors, excluding the occasional hand waving, chats over the fences, and borrowing of home and garden tools. Omak had specialists conduct an in-depth photo survey of the Bey house and the neighbors' yards.

The woman, who had been identified as Ione, did not appear to be connected to Neah Bey's work as a government agent. Indeed, she apparently believed that her husband worked for a nonprofit agency that helped poor people around the world. Ione Bey had worked her way up the power pyramid of a national association of health-care providers, to where she was in charge of physician credentialing for the Pacific Northwest.

Omak sat back and thought anew of Neah Bey while shuffling through some papers. How good was this guy to shield his wife of thirty-some years, and keep her in the dark about his true employment? Omak had his computer run a search on what physician credentialing entailed. He stared at the results; it involved the collection of data about physicians that had international experience and education. It involved working with dozens of individual insurance providers, and on top of that, working with sometimes aloof and pretentious doctors. Omak's estimation of Ione Bey elevated. He reviewed Neah Bey's medical history on a hunch. Bey had been shot; stabbed; bitten; run over; captured at least twice, requiring rescue by U.S. Special Ops teams both times; and more. Omak wondered if Ione was not the brains of the operation.

Respect for Ione Bey aside, Omak set in motion another hit, this time directly aimed at the Beys in their house in West Seattle. It seemed to be an obvious target.

Ione rustled the bedcovers. Bey whispered, "I have to go out to the office for a bit. I'll be back in after I write some emails." Ione rolled over, and the gray cat walked on her like a professional lumberjack on a turning log. The cat looked at Bey and hissed at him for having disturbed them.

Bey clicked back in to the commlink. "I'm moving from the house to the backyard and office." Someone clicked twice for affirmative. From his special case, Bey took out his night vision monocular. "Status all targets, please."

There was a brief pause. "Target One is kneeling next to the hedge at Joyce's south property line. Target Two is still out front in the sedan, surveying the scene with night vision equipment. Targets Three and Four are now getting out of the pickup truck and arming themselves."

Bey slipped out the back door. "Target One has acquired you." Bey ducked and there was a slap of something hitting the doorframe. A screen of hops that had reached the second floor of the house provided Bey with adequate cover. He slowly moved the leaves and vines aside and stuck the monocular through them. Target One moved slowly across the alley on all fours. Bey heard a voice in his ear say, "I can get a shot on Target One, a kill shot. I need him to move about five feet to the right."

Bey clicked twice, then moved to his right and shook the photinia. Target One stood up, took two steps, and then slumped over in the alley. There was a slight crack when the bullet shattered Target One's skull.

Bey moved to the north side of the house. "I have lost Target Two on the north side of your house." Target Two and Bey found each other there by crashing into each other. Each locked the other's gun under an arm, so neither could shoot. They fought with feet and head butts. There is no such thing as a fair fight when you're fighting for your own life.

Target Two lashed out with his cocked elbow. Bey countered with an arm sweep and an elbow strike to the throat. Target Two blocked Bey and backhanded him in the face. They were still clutching each other's gun hands as Bey stepped back and Target Two came forward in pursuit. Target Two ran into Bey's Muay Thai knee slams, and it was his turn to step back. Bey advanced.

Target Two crouched and reached down for a knife in a sheath at his waist. Bey let go of his own gun, freeing his trapped arm. Target Two slashed across Bey's chest on the forward strike and tried to impale him in the neck on the reverse. Bey threw up his right arm to block the reverse and stuck Target Two in the eye with his left thumb. As the knife came back, it laid open about three inches on Bey's forearm. Bey stepped through and caught his opponent in the side with an elbow. In a spin, Bey threw all his weight into his other elbow and caught his target on the side of the head. Target Two staggered back, and this allowed Bey a precious second of time to get his own knife out. The grip was slippery from the blood fountaining out of his arm.

The commlink chattered in his ear, "God damn it, Good Guy is in a knife fight on the north side of the house!"

"Targets Three and Four are coming up Good Guy's walk."

"I have a shot on Target Three!"

"Take it."

"Target Four is spooked, and is coming around the north side of the house."

Target Two and Bey danced, blades slashing in and out. *Everyone gets cut in a good knife fight*, Bey thought.

There was a gasp, and the bushes rattled behind them. "Target Four is down." That left Target Two and Bey. They closed. Target Two was taller, thinner, and stronger; Bey was shorter, thicker, and meaner. Parry, thrust, stab, riposte, slash, cover, duck; sweat ran into Bey's eyes.

Bey tried to consciously think of his breathing: inhale, exhale, inhale, and exhale. People forget to breathe in times of stress and it impairs abilities. Target Two was holding his breath. Bey figured if he could outlast him for another minute then Target Two would be slower, less able to concentrate, less capable of attacking or defending. They circled on the narrow walkway. Ione turned on the upstairs bedroom light; this created a pool of luminosity around the men. Target Two was startled and stepped to his left. Bey threw up his left hand to the other man's face; Target Two tried to block it, forgetting that the knife was in Bey's right. Bey slammed the knife into Target Two's midsection, and he folded over. Bey stood over him and grabbed his hair and pulled his head back, "Who? Who are you? Who sent you?"

Target Two grimaced; the pain was draining him as quickly as the blood loss. Bey jerked on his hair again. The target tried to raise his hand with the knife in it. Bey's foot slammed down on it, severely cutting Target Two's fingers in the process. "Tell me what I want to know, or there won't be an ambulance for you."

Target Two gurgled the words, "There will be others." His body stiffened and then went limp. His eyes glazed, and his last ragged breaths escaped from him. He was dead. Bey turned to see what was going on behind him. His security contingent was around him; one guy was wrapping Bey's arm in a handkerchief. Bey had a few other slices here and there.

"Gee, boss, you just bring all kinds of excitement to the party," someone said from the darkness.

"We need to get you stitched up. I suggest that we go to your office to get you patched up enough to get you out of here without your wife finding out about it, and then we sew you up en route to the plane." It sounded like a good plan to Bey. He was a little winded. They found some first aid supplies in the office. Tall Guy loaned his shirt to Bey for when he kissed Ione good-bye. The wounds were beginning to really hurt. Within an hour of when the car carrying Bey pulled out of the alley, a cleaning crew was already on the scene, removing things quietly, swiftly.

Omak watched the scene play out from a car down the street, as much as the houses and vegetation allowed. Using a very sophisticated scanner, he was able to find the frequencies Bey's security umbrella used. The scanner had to feed the signal into a descrambler, so Omak heard what was happening almost, but not quite, in real time. Although Omak wasn't sure about some of the decoded slang, it was clear that he was on the right frequency. Then the radio traffic ceased abruptly. No one moved around the Beys' house or on the street. When he saw three broad-shouldered individuals escort Bey to a vehicle in front of the house, Omak knew his strike team had failed.

Omak could see Bey's profile as the car turned a corner and drove away. Omak reached under his vest and grabbed the handle of his automatic. For a brief moment, he thought of taking out Ione Bey while Neah was away. He stopped and considered that all of the security umbrella might not have driven away with Neah. He slipped the transmission into neutral and silently rolled down the slight slope, past the Bey residence and into the night.

Joyce called Ione the next day to talk about the prowler she thought she had heard. Joyce had decided to install a motion sensing light that very afternoon. And someone had spilled some sort of cleaning supplies in the alley.

Bey had been stitched together in a lot of odd spots, but never in an airport parking garage.

Selah met him at the door, and this time did not accost Bey in her usual manner. She led him straight to the study. Dr. Lucerne was waiting, looking frail and tired. She did not get up, and her handshake was weak and indecisive. Bey sat down and looked across at her. "What's up, Doctor?"

She had a sort of milky look to her eyes. "Oh, just old age acting up," she sighed. Bey sat silently, not accepting her words. "Oh, alright, I am dying more rapidly than what I thought. It seemed that we had things in remission, and now we don't. Pity for me. Pity for you, too. Now you'll have to do all your own thinking."

Bey was stunned. Though Dr. Lucerne was cranky and crude, she was nevertheless a genius, and supported the Will of the United States. It was an awkward silence.

"Well, you needn't start counting the silver just yet; I have some more months left in me." She paused and looked out through the bulletproof glass. "But not many more. We should start to work; do you have anything intelligent to bring to the table today?" Bey leaned over the desk and kissed her on the cheek. Then Selah brought them the Kleenex and some hot cider.

Dr. Lucerne handed Bey back the photos from their

previous discussion. "Okay, Stuffy, what do you see now that you have not seen before?"

Bey thumbed through the pictures. "And what is it that I am supposed to be seeing?"

She smiled and sipped her drink. "Stuffy, look through the pictures like a good boy, or I'll just have to kick your ass." He studied picture after picture. Bey looked at the clothes, the shoes, the hair, the landscape; everything he could think of, he commented about.

"No."

"Not that."

"Never that."

"Kind of a lame brain, aren't you, Stuffy?"

Bey admitted that his patience was wearing thin and that most likely she was right that he was not smart enough to catch what she considered obvious.

"Oh, you silly little boy. Here, and here, and here."

She pulled three pictures from the stack and took a red grease pencil and circled earrings, nose rings, finger rings, toe rings, necklaces, and bracelets. Well, Bey guessed he had a right to feel stupid and inadequate. It was as plain as the nose on his face, and he told the doctor as much. "Oh, no, Stuffy, your nose is your best part! Why, it's the rest of you that is just awful!"

"Gee, thanks Doc," Bey responded. "Somehow I don't feel better."

"Okay, we can make any sort of metal parts, and specifically, jewelry parts, out of any metal that you like. But what is the delivery system that we can employ?" Bey was still trying to gather his self-respect, at least a little of it.

"Gosh, Stuffy, far be it from me to tell you your business, but do you remember Georgi Markov?" The doctor shuffled through some folders in her ancient oaken and leather file cabinet.

Yes, Bey knew about Georgi Markov, Bulgarian defector, reportedly killed by the Bulgarian secret police on the streets of London. Markov was standing at a bus stop when he heard a small pop, as did others near him. He did not think anything of it, and only felt a small touch on his leg when a passerby brushed his leg with an umbrella. Markov died from ricin poisoning. The attending physician at his autopsy took some samples, and only because it was the most unusual thing he could find, cut off a small pimple on the back of Markov's leg. When the autopsy results were returned, and ricin was found in Markov's system, red flags went up. How did Markov get an overdose of one of the world's most dangerous poisons, for which there is no known antidote?

The London doctor went back to his only uninvestigated sample, the slice of pimple tissue. Under the microscope, he found a small metal pellet. Metal gets into the human body in any number of ways, and is often found in ironworkers, foundry workers, welders, or hobbyists. It was under a high-powered microscope that the pellet was found to have incredibly tiny holes drilled in it. A spectroscopic analysis revealed the truth. Markov had been shot in the leg by an umbrella gun. The gun fired a tiny pellet, a hundredth the size of a BB, into Markov, and it was the infinitesimal amount of poison contained in the pellet that killed him.

"Alright, I get it now. We take advantage of humankind's desire to look good by providing people with jewelry treated with chemical compounds designed to reduce sperm count and sperm motility and delay or halt ovulation for as long as the jewelry is worn. Right?" Bey hoped his answer was adequate, as he could not take much more of the doctor's sharp wit.

"Bingo, Stuffy, go to the head of the class!" Dr. Lucerne looked ten years younger. "Well, can you now guess what the next thing we do is? Hmmmm?"

Oh, hell, Bey thought; he had hoped he was off the hot seat. It clearly was a day for him to leap from the frying pan into the fire, several times. Dr. Lucerne handed him the pictures and directed Bey to be a good student and look through them again. It took him a while, but for this round he decided to write down a list of things that he had previously commented on so he would not have to listen to the doctor repeat, "Nope, not that, or that, missed again! You silly little boy!"

Finally, out of desperation, he shouted, "All I see in these pictures is a bunch of chicks with too much makeup on!"

The doctor looked at him and said, "Bingo, Stuffy."

Selah knocked on the door and made a point of walking up to Bey and then staring at her wristwatch. It only took him a second to figure out it was time to let the doctor rest and for him to contact the Smiths.

Bey received updates on the first five hundred thousand pounds of soap. It was all gone, and in some parts of the world, the product was being ordered, shipped, and used at twice the estimated rate. Bey called Pomeroy at Stellar Soap and ordered one million pounds. He called the printers and told them to order a corresponding run of soap boxes and have the boxes shipped flat to Stellar.

The Smith, LLC operatives in the Midwest told him that the warehouse had stockpiled the various chemicals in advance. In the next ten days, a shipment would be on its way to Stellar.

So far, they had washed and treated almost a million pounds of clothing before it left the United States. Bey typed out a brief outline of the jewelry program and asked the Smiths to get back to him with a list of resources in the next few days.

Ione answered the phone on the second ring when he called, somewhat oblivious to the time difference between them. "What are you still doing up? It must be after one in the morning there." So it was. He asked her how things were going around the house. "Oh, just great, the Bingens came over for a game of cribbage last night, you'll like them, he is a former Navy Seal and she works for the government as a customs inspector. And the night before, I went over to the Raymonds and had dinner with them. Ruby is a quilter! So we bored poor Sloan to death with quilter talk. He had to go to work on a project in his upstairs office, so Ruby and I just chatted along until about nine thirty. When do you think you will be home?"

They conversed as only people who have been married for over thirty years can. In closing, Ione said, "Oh, and Almira Bingen wants me to go out and look at some rural acreage with them this weekend. Even though they just moved in. Would you like to live on a farm?" Actually, after having spent several days on Dr. Lucerne's estate, Neah did find the idea appealing. Most likely, country living would reduce the number of knife fights he got into.

The next day found Bey and Dr. Lucerne finishing up with the jewelry program. Smith, LLC emailed Bey and the doctor a lot of information to consolidate. Bey was summoned to D.C. again. Dr. Lucerne looked tired, but still snappy. "Come over here and let me take a look at your shaving misadventures." They were in the kitchen having a slice of homemade coffee cake. Selah came out of her quarters with a first aid kit of impressive proportions.

"No, that's okay; I'll have a doctor take a look at it." Bey backed away from Selah and the impressive suitcase. To say that the silence was frigid would have indicated only half the truth.

"Since I am a doctor, I will take a look at it, Stuffy."

"Oh, sure, I was thinking of like, you know, er, ahh, there's no real way of backing out of this, is there?" Bey stammered.

"No, so sit down, and maybe if you behave, you'll get a lollipop to go with the black eye I'm going to give you. Sit still or nasty Dr. Lucerne is going to get a rubber glove out."

Bey sat still.

After she cut away the dressings that covered the five slashes, she found that only three required stitching. "Let's see, does this hurt?" She pulled the hair on the side of his head.

"Yes, that does hurt. What was the point of that?" He watched her hands closely as they puttered around his still raw injuries.

"Oh, that, it's just a doctor thing to do." She continued to fuss over the wounds.

He thought for a moment. "What kind of a doctor does that?"

She smiled at him and said, "A nasty one, Stuffy. You got this as a result of your work?" She pointed at a raggedy scar partially hidden by his undershirt. Bey nodded. "This happened before?" She finger-traced a scar on his other arm where a Chinese army officer had grazed him with an AK-47 round. "And this one over here?" A guard dog had bitten Bey when he was scaling a fence in Slovenia. His rescuers told him that there was three days of intense pain and suffering, and then the dog died. "And how about this one?" She pointed to his chest; foolishly, he looked down and got his nose tweaked.

The not-so-good doctor and Selah laughed with great gusto. "How long have you and Ione been married?" she asked as she expertly wrapped his wounds in fresh dressings.

"Am I applying for a job here or what? Ouch!"

She slapped his arm over the big slash. She smiled. "Now, now. Answer the question or we'll play *turn your head and cough.*"

"Ione and I have been married thirty-six years, give or take two months. No kids, six cats. Anything else you want to know?"

Dr. Lucerne taped the end of the gauze off. "No, that will be all. You are a high-mileage high-maintenance sort of worker bee, aren't you?"

He put his arm back into his shirt and rolled his sleeve down. "Comes with the terrain, I guess. Every job has its hazards."

After he said good-bye to Selah, the doctor gave him a quick hug. There were tears in her eyes. "Take care of yourself, Stuffy. A good future depends upon your success." There were a few damp spots around Bey's eyes, too.

Omak turned on the computer, knowing full well that it was probably watching him the whole time. He sat quietly in front of the machine while it went through its startup processes. A message began typing across the screen. He punched the "escape" key, and the message stopped. Omak stared at the machine and said, "I know you can hear me. I won't be in contact for at least two months, maybe more. I'll call you." He then unplugged the machine, jerked the battery from the back, and fairly threw the laptop into a suitcase that he slid under the bed.

He had not run in months. He had not touched a weight in a gym in equally as long a time. By the time he had slogged three miles, he was covered in sweat and ached in every joint. He had a purpose, a mission, a desire, and he had to be in very good shape if he was going to be successful.

Omak rented a room in a small hotel-apartment in Williams, Arizona. He knew the high elevation would help him with his breathing as he jogged and rode a bike around town and out into the countryside. It was summer, and he was able to pay a few dollars a day to the janitor at the local high school for use of the weight room after hours. In his brain, and in his heart, Omak knew he was only healing the body, and nothing more.

Every now and then, he drove a few hundred miles in different directions and used a computer in a public library or coffee shop-internet café to send messages and get information. This he did sparingly and only if he was stuck on a particular problem. At one point, he asked for a team he could work with for a week or two. He asked for twice the number of team members he thought he needed. Casualties seemed to be high when confronting Neah Bey and his associates.

———————

The old man in the underground facility was highly agitated, and he vented his wrath-upon the men in the outer office. They were ordered to follow a specific line of thinking, then were stopped, told they had failed, and sent on another search. This action was repeated again and again until one of the young men failed to show up for his shift. He was found hanging in his closet. This meant that all the survivors would have to work harder and longer until a replacement could be found. That could take a while, since no one outside their little world knew they existed. Volunteers were not wont to walk through the door.

———————

From time to time, a brief message came in from Omak, asking about this town, this person, this company; his questions were odd and scattered. The young men tried to trace all of Omak's communications to find him, but to no avail. The young men cast glances at the door as smoke tendrils crept around its edges. Sometimes, they heard painful moaning and names recited in alphabetical order. Other times, they heard the old man laboriously pecking at his computer.

———————

They all jumped up from their consoles when three senior members of the Church arrived unannounced. Two of the three had missed being named pope by less than a handful of votes a few years previously. The highest-ranking member of the contingent stood outside the old man's door. He knocked and waited a respectful moment before opening the door. All three walked in. As the door closed, the last cardinal put his fingers to his lips, admonishing the men in the outer office to remain quiet. They could see that the old man had not risen from his chair as one would expect when senior members of the papal staff arrived to chat.

Omak ran and lifted weights. In two months, he had lost weight and restored his energy level to near normal. When he looked in the mirror at the high school, he saw what looked like fifteen years' worth of dark circles under his eyes.

Omak picked up a large express box at a mailbox shop in Peoria, Arizona. He had rented a fairly new motor home and was staying at the Paradise RV Park located near the junction of Peoria, Sun City and Surprise. It was filled with retired snowbirds. He avoided contact with them all, even one nice lady who reminded him of his late mother-in-law. She often stopped by and gave him a box of homemade cookies and a flyer for a nearby square-dancing club. He recycled the flyers and ate the cookies. In the box he had picked up were two dozen dossiers that Omak could sift through to select the men for his teams. After a few hours, he sent a message saying simply, "Hire them all." No response came back indicating anything, so Omak assumed he had all the men he needed.

He then began the process of subdividing the team into an A team and a B team. B was going to carry out the European hit, and A was going to hit Neah Bey. He chose the best to hit Bey. The rest were directed to meet in two months in a place north of London.

———

Tex was still there at the Smith House, managing the traffic flow and outside security. He opened the door for Bey this time and whispered, "You make us look bad when you get hurt, and you make us look worse when you do our job, so knock it off!" He shook Bey's hand, waited for the door to unlock, and held it open for him.

A new Miss Smith was behind the old desk. And a newer Miss Smith was sitting behind a new desk in the reception area. This made for a much larger kill zone should it come to that. Already a bead of sweat was forming at Bey's neck and beginning its familiar march down his spine.

One of the old familiar doors opened, and Bey walked in. The room behind the door was no longer an office; it was a modest-sized conference room. One entire wall was now a whiteboard. There were details of each of the current plans going forward at the present time on one half of the board. The other half was covered with details of the proposed work. Bey noticed that nearly seven million pounds of soap had been dispensed in half-pound boxes. The total affected population was in the millions.

Over three million pounds of treated clothing had left the docks in America. The tee shirt program was on track, producing fifty million shirts with the likenesses of Slick Watts, Ichiro, Edgar Martinez, Lauren Jackson, Bill Gates, and others.

The jewelry program was waiting on the manufacturer's production schedule. The trinkets were to be produced in China, Taiwan, and South Korea, and then shipped to the United States for "finishing."

Mr. and Mrs. Smith were sitting at the conference table. "Welcome, Stuffy, have a seat while we wait for the others. We trust your injuries are mending, not that we don't already know. The doctor has already checked in with us," she said, smiling at the reaction on Bey's face when she used Dr. Lucerne's nickname for him.

Bey sat and asked, "You are aware of the doctor's condition?"

There were nods at the other end of the table. "Yes, we are flying her back and forth from Sloan Kettering on a weekly basis. Her chances of living out two more years are slim, at best. You don't need to tell us. She is more valuable than any gem you can name. She is a feisty little gal."

The pain in Bey's arm where she had grabbed it to get his attention still throbbed. "Yes, although 'feisty' is not the word I would have chosen." He started to mouth a few of his favorite expletives, but was waved off by Mr. Smith.

"Yes, Bey, we get the idea." Mr. Smith frowned.

The rear door in the room opened. Another pair of Smiths came in. Bey had talked to only one of them before. One of the Mrs. Smiths started going over the material on the whiteboard.

There were never handouts. They reviewed the program. The conversation stopped briefly, and one of the Mrs. Smiths nodded to one of the Mr. Smiths. "You are a hot commodity right now. No one outside the organization seems to like you very much. There have been at least three attacks directed at you in the last year."

Bey got a little heated up and leaned forward. "I only know of two. Explain." The Smiths did not like being interrupted. *Too bad*, Bey thought.

"There was an incident near your house last evening. Ione is all right, and may not have been aware of the situation."

Bey stood up. "Spare me the roundabout and get to it, now!"

Heads snapped back, haughtily. "Two persons attempted to cut your wife out of traffic as she came home from the Metro Market on Admiral Way. Their attempt was unsuccessful. Her flankers did what they had to do, and both parties were terminated, one at the scene, the other later. Information was gathered."

Bey did not have to ask what that meant; he had been involved with information gathering before. "My wife is where?"

"Your wife is a strong-willed person; however, she and the 'Bingens' are now staying in Centralia. They are looking at rural property again. We would prefer that you consider moving to some acreage where we would be better able to cover you. The company will take care of building a new house and securing and monitoring the property as we do your current home. To facilitate this process, tomorrow your wife will find a nice seventy-five-acre parcel. She will fall in love with it." Mr. Smith's eyes narrowed. "And so will you."

Okay, a restful cottage in the country, sure, Bey thought. The value of staying in the house in West Seattle was diminished when Bey heard that Joyce's boobs were fakes, anyway.

———

Ione met him at baggage claim. The Bingens had offered to drive. For some reason, no one asked them not to park in the white zone. They shook hands all around, except Bey gave Ione more than one "I'm home" kiss.

On the ride home, Auburn Bingen told Neah about his job, something to do with actuarial activities with a national insurance company. This was a part-time consulting job. His wife, Almira, worked as a customs inspector at the Port of Seattle.

Ione had brought home several flyers on the real estate she and the Bingens had looked at. Bey said he was a little tired and just looked forward to taking a hot bath and relaxing. Bey did leaf through the flyers; one for seventy-five acres had a penned-in star in the upper right hand corner. Ione used that mark to note things of special interest. Seventy-five acres, rolling hills, two small pastures, big trees and a year-round creek; it all sounded good to Bey. His arm and ribs throbbed; he had forgotten to take a painkiller.

Bey sat out in the office, updating all his files. It was his and the Smiths' policy to work according to the "dead man" protocol. If Bey died today, had he left enough information behind to make the transition as seamless as possible? He used a synchronization wizard to download and upload files he stored on the Smith, LLC server.

The soap program was doing well, the tee shirt program was underway, and the treatment of the donated clothing was going to be a cornerstone of future operations. The jewelry was a coup of the first order.

His computer chirped and indicated that he had incoming mail. It was the report on the information gathered from one of the auto hijackers, along with other details of the investigation and autopsies of the deceased. The conclusion was not a happy one. Just as his organization was a ghost image of the government, there were other such ghost images of other organizations. The one that Bey had made an enemy of was the ghost of the Church.

The ghost organization of the Church was made up of the excommunicated, the deranged, the defrocked, the over-the-toppers, and some who were just devout believers. Everyone had an axe to grind, and some of the members used violence and evil to try to win back their souls in the eyes of the Church. Just as the conquistadors used the sword and the truncheon to spread the word of the Church, these outsiders used poison gas, murder, money, illegal arms, and more to gain a return to the Church and salvation. Bey estimated that he now had roughly one billion enemies. Cheery news for a rainy day. Odd how someone would use the very worst that humanity offered to try to achieve salvation.

Bey reached under the desktop and was comforted by the shrouded hammer Smith & Wesson .357 he had hidden there.

Didn't God help those who helped themselves? Or was he thinking of *do unto others*? Bey sighed and returned to his computer work.

Dr. Lucerne had sent him some emails on the jewelry process. After reviewing these, he forwarded them on to the Smiths.

The computer chirped again. This time it was a message from the home office. They had received the letter from Dr. Lucerne, which contained the chemical components needed to impact women's reproductive systems. Dr. Lucerne gave precise details as to the size of the chemicals at the microscopic level. This information led them to establish the correct sizing for the cavities need in the base metal of the jewelry. The doctor had attached a spreadsheet indicating different sizing requirements for earrings, finger rings, necklaces, and piercings. All had markedly different contact aspects with the human body. They were sending the information to an acquaintance of theirs that worked for GE Medical Systems. Bey would receive all relevant email updates in the future. One way to prepare the jewelry metal to absorb a chemical would be to blast away at the metal with accelerated particles. In a fairly brief period of time, the metal would be sufficiently pockmarked with miniscule indentations. These indentations would absorb the various chemicals.

Bey was also working on a project to soak donated footwear in a bath of their favorite chemical stew, building on the fact that the skin is a semi-permeable membrane. Bey remembered a tragic instance where children absorbed toxic material in their bodies by wading through what they mistakenly thought was clean running water.

Neah flew to L.A. and met with Pomeroy Gorst to see if Smith, LLC checks cashed and to tour the operation again. Gorst was very happy; in less than a year, Smith, LLC had become his tenth largest customer. He had come up with a plan to use Stellar Soap's other plants to speed up production and reduce shipping costs. Neah told him that this would be acceptable to them, but there was a hang-up that would have to be addressed. Pomeroy looked crestfallen. Bey slapped him on the back as they walked by a huge machine that was adding Styrofoam beads to the soap mix. The beads helped to fill the box, but cost less than the soap. "Pomeroy, it's just good news! Take it easy. Are the CEO and CFO here today?"

Bey already knew they were. Pomeroy looked even more uneasy, but said they were, and invited Bey to meet them. They all marched off to the second-floor conference room. They shook hands and chatted about the success of the Smith, LLC products around the world. Smith, LLC was having an impact already, but probably not what Stellar envisioned.

"Pomeroy mentioned the use of the other plants in the Stellar Soap Company, and that's why we are here." Bey smiled broadly. "Gentlemen, I want to thank each of you for your employee's knowledge and dedication to us, the customer. Pomeroy here has been a fount, an absolute fount of knowledge." Bey took a sip of water. "Well, today Pomeroy has broached the subject of using other Stellar Soap plants to reduce our costs and speed production. We are very happy to hear that this is possible, and we agree. With one small proviso."

The CEO and CFO looked pained, the CEO more so. Pomeroy looked near death. "We have a saying at Smith, LLC when dealing with other companies: 'Find the one person who makes a difference and focus on them.'" Bey smiled at each one of them. They had a lot of sayings at Smith, LLC, like, "Shoot 'em once in the belly and twice in the head, better one story, leave them dead," and other unhappy little bedtime tales. "So, we will proceed with Pomeroy's plans, with the condition that Pomeroy be the sole coordinator of this operation. I don't want my people having to call a dozen of your people; we just want to talk to Pomeroy. If there is a problem, we expect to contact Pomeroy and get it resolved. I suppose this means Pomeroy will have to get a bigger office, a fancy car, and a new title and salary to give him the power he needs to have the necessary clout. And we understand his promotion might impact our costs a little. However, if we spread the cost out over the next order of two million pounds, we should both benefit from this co-venture. Right?"

Pomeroy was ready to bust his buttons, and the two other gentlemen were slowly unwinding from their possible coronaries. *And Pomeroy will think that Smith, LLC is the salt of the earth*, Bey thought, smiling.

Ione called Neah as he drove the rental car to John Wayne. "Did you have a chance to look at the real estate sheets like you promised? The agency called and wanted to know our status."

Let's see, the Smiths on one side and the wife on the other. *I'm going to lose either way*, he grumped.

"You know, honey, the larger piece, what was the size of that?" He heard some paper rustling.

"That would be the Thompson Creek Farm, seventy-five acres. Two pastures, big trees, solitude, and no Joyce to distract you." Was he ever going to get a break on that?

"Oh, yeah, that's it! If you like it, honey, then call that

agent back and tell him we'll sign on the dotted line this weekend."

Ione asked, "Can we afford it? Can we really afford it? It would be wonderful! Building our own home, wide open spaces, nearer my family and all that." Whether Bey could afford it or not was beside the point. Ione wanted it and that was that. Bey opened the small journal he carried and found the check that the Smiths had given him; it seemed to cover the cost of the land and a substantial portion of any building they might have to do.

What the hell. "Not a problem, honey, I got a bonus that should arrive shortly and that should take care of part of it."

Ione sounded happy to be leaving the city and moving closer to her family. That was okay with Neah all the way around, and with the Smiths, too. Ione would have a nice, well-built house near her family, a sizeable bank account, and several more benefits that she was unaware of. Bey shrugged noting that so few of the agents live to retirement age anyway. Bey wondered what the retirement age was, come to think of it.

———

Pomeroy called from California. He wanted Bey to come down and talk something over. *Odd, so few people enjoy my company that much. Oh, well,* he shrugged, *off to California.*

Ione and Neah took the train down, and splurged on the private cabin. It was wonderful watching the scenery glide past. Bey had not been on a train in years. When he was a child, his mother took him from California to Illinois. They stayed at her family's farmhouse, and then they took the train to Washington State. His dad had driven north and purchased a house, as his job had moved. He remembered being lulled to sleep by the clickety-clack of the wheels on the rails. Not anymore—the rails were all welded together now.

They ate in the glass-roofed cars, and played cards and chatted with other travelers. They picked up a rental Corvette from an agency near the train station and zipped around with the top down. The Beys laughed and smooched in public. The hotel was ready for them, and they took a walk along the waterfront before retiring with room service for dinner.

Bey dropped Ione off at a quilting symposium for the day, and fussed through traffic to get to Stellar Soap in south L.A. His sat phone rang.

"Hello? May I help you?"

"This is Tex. Yeah, I know what you call me behind my back. Watch your ass down there, we got problems."

Bey could hear a muffled boom. He could hear Tex shouting, "Son of a bitch, what was that? An RPG? Jesus, here in town?" There was another boom.

"Like I said, watch your ass, things are heating up. We just took the safeties off the camera guns." Bey could hear the rattling buzz of the minis as they wound up, shut down, and wound up again. Sirens approached in the background.

"Are you guys all right? Do you need me to do something?" Bey asked.

There was some more small arms fire. "Okay, that was a close one. Everybody all right?" Tex had set the phone down; Bey could hear shell casings dropping near the phone as someone racked off five fast rounds. "Son of a bitch, where did that guy come from?" There were distant shouts. "They blew a hole in the fence and drove in? Okay, everyone smoke 'em if you got 'em. And smoke 'em if you see 'em."

There was a scraping sound, and the phone connection became laden with static. "Okay, you still there?" Bey assured Tex that he was. "Well, we got word that the fanatics were going to try something. They hit us in London and here in the last hour. No casualties on our side. The bad guys got their asses kicked. I think we've got seven bad ones ready for the Ziploc here, and about four in London."

Bey asked, "What was the tip? How did you know?"

Tex stopped for a minute and his breathing calmed. "They faxed us a picture of you and your wife when you were on the train. It was taken from the outside. It was a two-part picture. One of you and your wife riding along at sunset, then the near-ground shot of the back of a guy's head holding a LAW rocket aimed at your sleeper cabin."

Bey's heart sank as he wondered, *Where was Ione, right now?*

"Uhhh, is your wife with you?"

Bey swallowed hard, "I left her at the quilting symposium at the exhibition building near John Wayne Airport." Neah's mind went blank.

"Has she got a phone, can you call her?"

"I'll have to hang up and call."

Tex shouted, "No, do not hang up! What is the number? I'll call from here on another line."

Bey rattled off the number, and Tex repeated it back to him. "Hang on, I'm dialing. It's ringing. Hello? Ione? Yes, I'm so very sorry to be disturbing you at the quilting symposium. I'm Tex from your husband's company. No, we haven't met. I look forward to it soon. Yes, I've just gotten off the phone with him. He wants you to stay inside at the symposium, stay in a crowd. Yes, it's all very melodramatic. Unfortunately, there has been a threat issued against one member of the company. No, not your husband specifically. No, there is really nothing to worry about. Your husband will be back there just as soon as he can. Ione? Yes, I am sending one of my security personnel over to stay with you. No, no problem at all. The security person is named Ravenna Lakota. She will show you her identification card. Yes, I'll get back in touch with you if anything happens. Ravenna will find you, so there is no problem with going back to the classroom. Yes, thank you very much."

Bey could hear the receiver being set back down. "Sheesh, you train your wife to ask that many questions?"

Bey tried to laugh. "What the hell is going on, Tex?"

"We got this email of the pictures via a public computer located in a library in Soho. Half an hour later, the Thames office got hit with small arms fire and some homemade pipe bombs. It tore the place up, some injuries on our side. The Limeys were able to gather information from one of the survivors of the attacking force. The part where I told your wife you weren't the target? I lied. You *are* the target."

Bey pulled into the gated area of Stellar Soap. Even though it was a Wednesday, the parking lot was vacant.

"Yeah, I figured that out myself. I'm in the parking lot at Stellar, and you'd think the place was closed."

"Well, get the hell out of there!"

Bey stomped on the gas and started to do a passable drifting one-eighty. The windshield of the 'Vette fractured into a crazy pattern of tracings and then exploded into thousands of small pieces, some of which sliced up Bey's face. He straightened the wheel and allowed the tires to smoke. The shooter was near the front door, and if Bey went out the way he came in, he'd go under the gun's muzzle again.

Unfortunately, a semitrailer blocked the back gate. Bey put the 'Vette into reverse, backed up the loading dock, and smashed through the thin metal garage door. This was a bad move. The door obscured his vision until a roof beam ripped it off the top of the 'Vette. Bey guessed that buying the supplemental insurance for the car had been a wise business decision.

The brakes barked hard on the slick floor of the plant. Bey got a quick lesson in soap properties; they make the floor very slick. Bey quickly estimated that the 'Vette suffered about ten grand in body damage as it scraped along a mixing machine. The car stopped, and Bey grabbed his case from the backseat. The top compartment looked like the inside of a briefcase; a bottom compartment held a partially disassembled MP5. It took a few seconds for Bey to slap the stock on and jam the magazine in. He threw the silencer back into the area behind the front seat. Bey thought slamming into the overhead door and smoking the tires on the factory floor made using the silencer something of a moot activity.

Bey was rewarded for his subtlety by having a bullet snip the upper part of his left arm. At least it was a new wound and would not interfere with the healing of the knife slashes. Bey crawled out from behind the 'Vette and scampered over to a passageway behind some heavy soap machines. There was a clang as a bullet shattered off a large hydraulic cylinder. Fluid began spraying out over a wide area. There was clang, and another bullet ricocheted off of one of the steel beams holding the roof up.

Rolling to his right and looking under the machine, he could see a pair of legs shuffling behind one of the machines about fifty feet down the production line. Bey was at a disadvantage: it was not his plant, it was not his turf, it was not his city, and it was not his state. A close shot scattered some bullet and steel fragments into his right leg. Clearly, it was also not his day. He rolled again.

This time, Bey could look down the small lane that separated the rows of machines. He saw the shooter stand up and rather unsteadily raise a rifle. It was Pomeroy Gorst. "Hey! Pomeroy! Knock it off! Let's talk this over!" For the first time, Bey noticed a silence in the factory. As his hearing returned to normal, he heard the faint hiss of fluid jetting onto the floor to his right.

"I can't stop! Don't you see? I'm part of this whole thing you did!" To add some emphasis to his statement, he touched off a round that was wide to the right.

"Pomeroy! I don't care what happened. We can protect you from whoever is making you do this." Bey could see Pomeroy trying to figure out where he was. His head twisted back and forth.

Pomeroy continued shouting. "Did they fire you? Did they close your plant? Did they lay off all your friends? That's why we are here! The people found out and bought us out and shut us down!" Bey moved back, trying to remember the layout of the plant based on his brief tour.

"Pomeroy, we can hire you, we can start another plant! It will all work out!" Pomeroy apparently did not believe what Bey was saying and shot close to his position. Again, splatter from the round slapped into Bey. And it really, really hurt. "Who did this to you? Who bought the plant?" Another shot hit close by. Bey was going to have to change tactics. He was getting tired of being turned into Swiss cheese.

"You know who," Pomeroy yelled. "They said you'd know, they called themselves a lot of things."

Oh, great! Bey grimaced with clenched teeth. His arm had started to bleed again. These guys really thought that God was on their side, and maybe they were right.

Another round slammed into something above Bey. "Pomeroy, God damn it, stop doing that!" Bey was turning to his left to belly crawl to a spot behind a huge machine for drying soap flakes when a round hit near his left thigh. Concrete exploded, sending bullet fragments and concrete chips into Bey's leg. The leg was getting to be very messy. Bey could look down and see a matted patch of torn pants leg holding a football-sized patch of flesh together. And Bey learned something else about soap. Soap burns in open wounds.

"Pomeroy, stop and think for a second! We can make a deal!" The next round went right by Bey's ear in reply. Bey rolled over onto his back and looked up, trying to formulate a plan.

There were all sorts of pipes running across the ceiling. Someone had thoughtfully marked each one. Hot water, cold water, wastewater, fire sprinkler water, natural gas, and roof drain. He did not care about any of the pipes, except the one marked "natural gas"; it was about four inches in diameter. He traced it back as far as he could see. There were all sorts of smaller pipes branching off of it. The four-inch must be the main. Bey squeezed under some machines, vowing to eat less of Ione's Key lime pie in the future.

Pomeroy must be having some difficulty tracking me, Bey thought. Pomeroy's job would be easier when he found the blood trail. Bey found the main shutoff for the huge dryer. Adjacent to the valve was a control box that said "Flame Detector" and "Pilot Light." It took some doing, but Bey managed to turn the valve all the way off. He opened the box and shorted the flame detectors so that the furnace would operate without being turned on. He pulled the relays for the pilot light supply.

Pomeroy was persistent and seemed to have an endless supply of ammunition. Bey supposed that if your future held the promise of eternity in hell, then you would plan your redemption out fairly well. *Damn,* thought Bey. He could hear Pomeroy shuffling.

"I see your blood here; let me take your pain away. We will pray for you and your soul."

"Thanks for reminding me," Bey whispered to no one. His vision was getting a little blurry as he struggled to tolerate the pain in his thigh. Bey started to turn the main valve back on, hoping that he had kept it off long enough for the pilot lights to burn the gas out of the main. With the flame detectors out of commission, and the pilots out, the flow would begin filling the dryer with unburned gas. It was time to head towards the door. If the gas exploded, Bey would not need the door at all. His ashes would rain down on greater L.A. for months to come.

Slim satisfaction, in my lowly estimation. Bey winced and wished he hadn't left his case with his pain pills in the wreckage that was once a sixty-thousand-dollar American-made sports car.

Bey got into a crouch and sprinted to the nearest wall, and fell against it. Looking to his left, he saw nothing. Looking to his right, the happy green glow of an exit sign was only fifty steps away. Fifty steps in the open with scant more than those flimsy-looking cardboard drums to act as cover. Bey supposed saying a prayer would be hypocritical to say the least. However, he dredged one up just as an insurance policy. One last chance for Pomeroy. "Pomeroy! Put down the gun! I promise we can work this out! It's not your fault! Those people who have caused this are misguided fanatics. They have attacked two government installations already today. Don't be another of their victims. Don't be a victim of a lie!" Bey grimaced in pain at the irony of his remarks. Everything that Bey had done on his population project was a lie. There was silence; Bey could not hear any steps. Hopefully, Pomeroy was thinking it over.

A splinter of metal gouged up by a bullet drilled itself into his side, just above the belt line. Pomeroy was apparently not going to play along. Bey ducked and ran, and discovered that the metal splinter had dug a little deeper than he had originally thought. He fell and crashed into the drums. It was a form of human bowling, with Bey the ball and the empty containers the pins. It would have been a little more helpful if some of the drums were full—then they would have at least offered some protection from the hail of bullets that Pomeroy sent Bey's way. Pomeroy was an amateur, and committed amateur mistakes.

Aim, then fire. Bullets don't guide themselves after they leave the barrel. Bey remembered an instructor admonishing him with those words many years ago. Pomeroy's inexperience was Bey's only luck of the day.

He got to the door and fell against the panic hardware as Pomeroy started to get his weapon under control. "Pomeroy! Last chance!" The shooting stopped. Bey aimed his gun towards the open maw of the dryer and shifted it from three round burst to full auto.

With a sobbing voice Pomeroy cried out, "Don't you think I know that?" The wire glass in the door shattered. Bey started to fall backwards through the door and was outside when he pulled the trigger. He rolled as fast as he could and fell off the raised part of the loading dock as the entire building left the foundation.

He kept rolling and crawling away from the inferno; his clothes felt white hot against his skin. He rolled some more and said a silent thank you to his wife for outfitting him in natural fibers and not some plastic crap that someone would have had to peel off in an emergency room, taking his skin with it.

Bey was pelted with all sorts of debris: roofing, piping, flaming parts of this and that. He got a very nice lump on his head from some steel fitting from the dryer. He sat up and admired his handiwork. A craftsman should always take pride in his work. Pomeroy would have been proud of his. It seemed that the metal splinter was now more in Bey's body than out. When you get stung or hurt your body gives you a few moments of an almost dreamlike state of wellbeing, with almost no pain. Bey had been in this position before. He grabbed the splinter and pulled it out.

Typically you should leave impaling foreign objects as they are found. This one was hampering Bey's mobility. Somewhere in the distance, there were sirens. The angry black cloud of smoke that rose from the wreckage filled the Southern California sky. It was going to be difficult for Bey to explain that he had really had nothing to do with this, as long as he sat in the parking lot of the building that had just exploded. With a variety of wounds and burns all over him, and a machine gun draped around his neck. There was a loud secondary explosion that sent a fireball a hundred feet into the air. Bey figured that there was going to be a lot of extra paperwork required to explain to the car rental agency just what happened to their 'Vette. He fell to the side, his head cracking against the pavement.

———————

Someone was calling his name from above. God? Was he that far gone? The sunlight dimmed, and it was not because of the smoke. That was blowing nicely into a major shopping mall and residential area. Bey really liked doing things up right. Someone was still calling his name, and it was getting windy.

Oh, it's a helicopter trying to squish me into the pavement. Bey's eyes swam with pain, and he vomited up a shirt full of bile. There was an angel flying out of the chopper to take him too, huh? This was no angel; this was a guy in black coveralls smoking a cigar. He shouted Bey's name, and Bey nodded. "I'm a friend of Tex's! He said to take care of you and Ione!" The roar of the chopper was diminishing, along with Bey's vision. The angel that needed a shave gave him a bear hug and tied a strap under his armpits, and then they flew, up and away into oblivion.

Bey was tossed to the floor of the chopper and looked

up to see Ione. She looked more like an angel than Tex's friend did. He passed out.

Omak swore and threw pots, pans, anything he could lay his hands on around the RV. He was watching the Soho hit work out as planned. The team did as expected, and actually got further into the compound than he thought they would before being eradicated by the European arm of the Smiths. He had hoped for much better results from the Washington, D.C., hit. The big men working for the Smiths went from looking like gentle uncles and older brothers to acting like enraged animals. Omak stared at the screen as the imaging panned frantically left and right.

"God damn it, don't they ever miss?" Even after getting knocked off their feet by the RPGs, the men jumped up and reacted to the incoming gunfire. They ran towards the sounds of the muzzle blasts. Omak's men withered and died in the street, on the adjacent rooftops, and in the armored vans that quartered the intersection. The person holding the camera fell down, and the lens cracked. Still, the camera transmitted the audio and video signal. A man with short gray hair walked up and appeared to look at the person behind the lens. The camera wiggled as the downed man tried to move. The gray-haired man kicked the camera around so it showed the face of Omak's team leader. A muzzle of a large bore handgun came into the frame. A deafening report from the gun killed the microphone. The video signal turned red, and then faded away. Omak sat down and turned the computer off. He then placed it in the oven of the RV. Omak began going through the last of the dossiers of his A team, and vowed to be there when the last hit was made. He was going to make sure of its success *personally.*

Sadly, it appeared to Bey that he had died. Two minions of the Dark Lord were complaining and being rude nearby. His head swam and flew through a hazy cloud. *If this is hell, they probably have some killer drugs here.* Bey tried to smile. Drool ran out of his mouth. The scene brightened a bit, and the two arguing minions came into better focus. The minions were calling for investigations and were stabbing someone in the back, most likely literally the way it sounded. He seemed to float upwards, and the scene got brighter still. It was then that Bey's hearing started to mesh with his brain. Slowly, a veil was lifted from his eyes. He probably wasn't in hell after all; the minions were Kudlow and Cramer on CNBC.

He was sort of half sitting up. There were people standing near the bed and seated around the room. Bey's right arm was strapped onto some kind of a board and there were tubes poked into his skin. He hurt just about everywhere, but the drugs kept him from feeling more than he could stand. Time seemed to run backwards and forwards at the same time. People were talking and having coffee. His throat was dry, and there were pieces of plastic stuck up his nose.

Bey arched his back and tried to get up and away from all of it. Hands came from the foggy areas in his peripheral vision and pushed him back, gently. "Honey, the doctors want you to lie still all of today and most of tomorrow." It was Ione. Then this could not be hell, even if Kudlow and Cramer were here. Then how could it be heaven if Kudlow and Cramer *were* here? He sank back, and darkness enveloped all that was of his universe.

The next time he started to drift towards the surface he was better able to process information. Apparently someone had read his file and realized that he couldn't take any sort of muscle relaxants or pain medication, except in miniscule quantities. He was in a hospital. He had been in hospitals before. Normally he walked away after a few hours or so. He did not feel like walking anywhere right now. There was a cramp in his left side. Spots on his arms and legs alternated between aching dully and feeling like they were being burned with hot coals. He wanted some aspirin in the handy gallon-sized bottle.

This time he could make out the people in the room: Ione, Tex, Selah, Dr. Lucerne, Dreadlocks, Tall Guy, and one of the Smiths. They were all staring at him. "Okay, so would someone get me a drink of water, please?" That was what he wanted to say; what really came out was a series of squeaks, gargles, and gasps.

Dr. Lucerne spoke up first. "That'll be the smartest thing he's said in months." Everyone laughed. Except Bey. "Oh, alright, give the whining little boy some juice and we'll see if that brings him around some."

Selah was kind enough to pour a glass, and Ione held it out in front of him. Lesson one: hearing Kudlow and Cramer when you think you are dead does not indicate that you are in hell. Lesson two: those who are healthy will always make fun of those near death's door. Lesson three: don't try to grasp a glass of juice with your right hand when the right hand has needles stuck in it.

He took a few sips of cran-apple juice. It was iced and cold, his favorite. The liquid washed away the crud in the back of his throat and carved a river of cool all the way to his stomach. He cleared his throat. "What happened after the building blew up?"

Tex spoke. "Well, we had Ravenna Lakota escort your wife to the roof of the quilting exhibition hall, and we flew to where you were conducting some sort of massive urban renewal project. Without a permit, we hear."

Ione was holding his left hand. "You are such a busy, secretive person, how come you never told me any of this?"

Bey looked at Mrs. Smith, who said, "Your husband's work is of the utmost importance to the United States. It is secret work and is, as you now can personally attest, some-times dangerous. He has never been allowed to discuss this with anyone, even with you."

The room was silent for a bit as Ione digested this in-formation. Dr. Lucerne leaned forward. "You are kind of clumsy, aren't you? I brought a whole box of rubber gloves in case you don't behave. These are the really long ones that go all the way to my elbow. You know the kind." She straightened. "Okay folks, it's time we all left Fireball here to mend. Let's go get something to eat." Dr. Lucerne looked at him and asked, "What is your favorite meal?"

He thought for a second and said, "Roast beef, with Yorkshire pudding, mashed potatoes with the red skins left on, creamed corn, a small salad, and homemade ice cream with lots of chocolate sauce."

Dr. Lucerne smiled the whole time. "That sounds just terrific, and I know just the place for all of us to go and get some. It will be wonderful telling your wife all about your career. But you'll have to stay here and sip your juice like a good little boy, while we eat like queens and kings. Let's go!"

Dr. Lucerne is an evil little woman, thought Bey.

Dreadlocks stayed in the room, sitting in a chair with his commlink on, reading the London *Times*. When everyone else had exited, Bey saw there were two other people standing outside the room. Bey dozed off.

Ione and Neah went back to the Caribbean island with Dr. Lucerne and Selah. Bey was healing, still a little stiff on his left side, but almost back to fighting trim. Dr. Lucerne tortured him every day, looking at dressings, poking, prodding, and taking stitches out. Selah was something of a physical therapist and masseuse all rolled into one. Bey liked the back massages she gave him twice a day. However, Bey did not like having to do sit-ups and leg lifts with her barking at him to do more.

On the veranda, they worked on their own projects. Ione was now part of the team. She handled the internet searches for data and all the correspondence for them. Selah was the go-to girl for all the supplies. Tex, Dreadlocks, and Tall Guy always hovered around. Bey didn't think they ate or slept at all. He was finally introduced to Ravenna Lakota when she flew in to help round out the security flankers. She and Ione had hit it off right from the start.

When Ravenna extracted Ione from the quilting exhibition and symposium, one guy tried to interfere with the process. He was an agent of the opposition, but a poor one, and slow. So slow that Ravenna was able to break his arm in two places and partially crush his trachea with an elbow strike. He was able to supply additional information prior to his fatal cardiac arrest.

―――――――

The buzzer sounded faintly, and the young men in the outer room grimaced as if in pain. Palix thought that being called into the presence of the old man three times in one week was extreme. He had been the point person for running Omak, so he was aware of all the plans that had been made. The knock was like before, briefly filled with hope that the occupant had changed his mind about the audience. Such was not the case. The room was filled with a stinking cloud of smoke that made his eyes water. He had once politely suggested that a fan and better ventilation be installed to clean the air. The old man rebuffed him with a stern look and said, "It is penance."

The old man stared at Palix, who as always stared above his head. The old man smiled inwardly, enjoying the visual cues of fear: pulse throbbing at the neck, perspiration forming on the upper lip, and eyes darting to and fro instead of being fixed at the usual point about a foot over his head. He waited, knowing this put the younger man in even greater discomfort. Eventually he spoke. "You have been faithful. In spite of your earlier transgressions, shall we say?" He paused, letting the words open old wounds. The pulse quickened and the sheen of perspiration spread across the face. "Now is the time you decide if you are worthy of heaven." The old man slid an envelope across his desk.

―――――――

Ravenna taught Ione some basic self-defense moves. In slow times, she, Ione, and Tex went off into the palm groves to shoot. Bey knew they were having a good time of it as the types of firearms changed and the rate of fire increased. Bey was a little concerned when, while out taking a stroll, he came up on Tex holding a coconut in the palm of his hand while Ione used Neah's prized .45 Auto to place one shot into it from twenty feet out.

"That sort of pisses me off, you know," Bey grumbled under his breath.

Bey was now up to three bouts of Selah beating the tar out of him per day. Sit-ups, leg lifts, treadmill, stair climber, weight machine, exercise cycle, and his all-time favorite, walk/jog in loose sand. Not down in the packed stuff where it would have been easy, no, not that.

Regarding their special "Cleanliness is next to godliness" soap project, they had hard evidence that in the thirteenth month of the soap program, they were actually getting results. Their evidence was based on birthrates , prenatal insurance claims, and orders for baby clothing. It was working. It was working well enough that they could hand that part of the program off to a special group of Smith, LLC personnel who were trained to run with operating programs. They took no offense in being relieved of that portion of their project. It was part of the process; those who get the company going are not necessarily those who keep the company going. They had to start up another part of the program.

Ione had compiled a detailed search of all well drillers in the areas of the world that the project was focusing on. She was refining her search to distinguish oil and gas and other mineral drillers from those that drilled for water. Water well drillers worked in three general areas: industrial uses, agricultural uses, and potable water supplies. Sometimes the same person or company did work in all three areas, and other times they specialized in just one. Bey, Dr. Lucerne, and Ione then worked through a list that included the UN and other governmental agencies that were suppliers of funds to these drillers for the creation of water supplies. Ione then came up with the notion that there might be a lot of charitable companies working towards small potable supplies for tiny villages here and there. They ended up with a list of ninety-eight thousand eight hundred and sixty-four drillers that in some part supplied potable drinking supplies to about a quarter of the world's population.

Dr. Lucerne refused to let Bey leave the island and claimed that he should have four more weeks of rest and recuperation before being allowed to travel. "He is just barely able to perform any meaningful activities, such as going to the bathroom, dressing himself, and eating." She was talking to Smith, LLC Headquarters in Washington, D.C., on a sat phone. She listened. "Oh, you mean that this was his condition before the 'accident'? Then how will we know he is ready to leave and carry on with his life's work? He slobbers, eats with his fingers, and has a thing about breasts, especially those of someone named Joyce. Oh! I had no idea that is normal for him." Dreadlocks and Tall Guy thought that this was the funniest thing they had ever heard, and were howling with laughter for days afterwards.

Bastards, Bey thought quietly.

Ione received reports about three times a week on the construction of the house—where it was at in the permit process, how many yards of concrete had been poured, how many feet of water and waste lines were being ordered or set in place. She had the contractor take digital pictures and email them. Smith, LLC employees were in many of these photos.

They had a conference between Dr. Lucerne, Ione, Tex, two of the Smiths, and Neah. A program was laid out that would provide a large percentage of the costs of drilling of any new wells for potable water. They focused on the smaller areas, the more remote areas, and areas least likely to be able to perform tests on the water supply.

Ione interrupted, stating, "If that's an issue, why not have the village matriarch take the sample and send it to us? We then could do the usual screen for contaminates and dutifully report on those and neglect to mention the additives. We should do this for free."

One, it was a brilliant idea. Two, Bey thought he was going to have to restrict Ione's contact with the not-so-good doctor. Dr. Lucerne appeared to be having a negative impact on his wife. Three, as always, Bey was very proud of his wife.

Mr. Smith looked at the whiteboard, then made a few scribbles on his slate and showed these to Mrs. Smith, who nodded in agreement. He stood along with Mrs. Smith and said simply, "Agreed. Done. We are leaving. Good-bye."

After their chopper took off, Dr. Lucerne came over and gave Ione a hug. "Why that was brilliant, Ione, just brilliant! Moreover, your strategy does not require the use of bombs, poisons, murder, or guns. So naturally, the idea would never occur to what's-his-name over there."

Dr. Lucerne smiled at Bey. Selah smiled at him too, and

Tex, Dreadlocks, and Tall Guy laughed at him. Bey gave them the finger.

They were flying out to the first well site that local village elders were inaugurating. The tribe had been drinking river water that was so horribly polluted that disease and early death were rampant. Bey did not think for even a second that improving the cleanliness of the water was counterproductive to their efforts. Everyone should have the ability to drink clean water and not get intestinal parasites, dysentery, or any of a dozen other maladies. The villagers were going to be a lot better off, but with a lower birthrate than before. They would actually benefit; the children would not suffer from drinking water filled with industrial wastes and raw sewage.

Tex and Bey inspected the well, pointing out pipes and valves and power supplies. It was not much of a task; a hole in the ground had been drilled to a safe depth. A steel casing had been installed with a sand point at the bottom. A small pump and associated piping had been lowered into the well, and this was all connected up to a manifold of hose bibs. Simple. Someone had taken into consideration the watering of animals and the resultant piles of dung in the vicinity. There was a concrete pad around the top of the well, and the watering manifold was located at least two hundred feet from the wellhead itself. The manifold was located at the bustling intersection of Malaria Way and Jesus-look-at-the-size-of-that-cockroach Boulevard.

The local government (or what passed for that) installed good karma at the outlets. There was much singing, dancing, and spraying of the crowd from a garden hose, and the first important pile of dung was deposited by a very tired looking ox. Smith, LLC guaranteed that the well would do what it was intended to do for three years. They hired the local facilities director to take a sample of the water every three months and send it to Smith, LLC. In the top of the wellhead, just under the flange, was a small cavity built into the pipe. It held what, for all intents, looked like a fancy stainless steel strainer. In fact, it was a strainer that had to be replaced once a year. Smith, LLC technology was used to etch the metal used for the strainers and bind various chemicals to it; the strainers were designed to deliver a measured flow of the chemicals into the drinking water supply. This first well was one of two thousand wells being developed as part of at least five thousand two hundred and fifteen different aid projects.

When the priest and child abuse scandal rocked the Church, the Smiths were torn between joy and sorrow. The world could blame the Smiths for a lot of things, but they couldn't be blamed for that. So Bey was told.

The young man prayed silently at his computer console. The others in the room chose to keep their attention on their own work. Sweat trickled down the sides of his face and ran along the stubble of his beard until it dripped from the point of his chin. After a few minutes, he opened the envelope, read its contents, and left the room without comment. In his austere quarters, he lay on his bed and sobbed uncontrollably into his pillow.

The Smiths had replaced the Stellar Soap Company with another provider. The disaster in L.A. was blamed on faulty gas piping. The exact set of circumstances surrounding the closure of the plant and the associated closure of the rest of the company was never known. The money trail pointed to a subsidiary organization that offered an incredible amount of money for the purchase of all of Stellar. The board of Stellar was handed a number of checks that were all good. Then a new board was installed, and the company closed one afternoon. Smith, LLC sources indicated members of the old board were impressed with the notion that staying away from the soap business meant staying alive. Stellar's closure caused a dip of slim significance in the program.

Bey was now fully recovered from his injuries. Dr. Lucerne spent half her time living with the Beys and the other half living on her estate. Selah was her constant companion, and Bey enjoyed the occasional back rub when her duties permitted. Selah had the hands of a grizzly bear, and the deep tissue manipulations felt great, tearing out the scar tissue in some spots.

Tex was assigned to Dr. Lucerne as the head of her security detail. Tall Guy was security chief for the Beys, and Dreadlocks came in when Dr. Lucerne arrived for a visit.

Ione seemed to thrive in this new environment. She practiced her self-defense work with Ravenna, and her shooting with whoever was handy. Ravenna became a regular visitor to the Beys' new residence, which Dr. Lucerne dubbed Compound Fracture. She pointed at Bey and said, "And we all know why." Bey frowned. Ravenna made travel arrangements for all concerned, and ran a network of listeners.

The listeners are the part of the gray government that people should fear the most. Each and every one of the population is a listener, to some degree. People comment at lunch, and someone listens. Someone posts an email, and someone else reads it and forwards it on. Citizens read a newspaper article from some small town, and it gets cut out and sent along. The most effective listening networks are a variety of news clipping services. They can be found listed in the Yellow Pages or online. One time, an astute politician told Bey that two years before you announce that you are running for office, you must begin collecting all the articles you can on all your potential adversaries. You'll find all the dirt you need to sink them.

Ravenna carried with her a rather elaborate computer and sat uplink. Her clipping services all emailed their findings to her. She spent most of her time reviewing, editing, and sending in data for further processing. She was well-suited for the work as she could speak and read five languages. One of her assignments was to read everything that was being written about population figures in approximately thirty countries. Anything that was written on the subject that even hinted something was in or out of line or even just normal crossed her screen. The whole team could use this fairly real-time data stream to tweak various programs.

She also ran a calendar program that advised her in advance of the holidays or special events of each country, religion, family group, or tribe. The Smiths then reduced the price of jewelry to augment gift-giving on certain occasions. The price of soap fell before festivals so that all the clothes would be washed. Information on where to emphasize the drilling of safer wells was derived from disease rates. Money was sent to fund regular birth control methods and family planning education efforts when and where the local population was receptive, which sadly was not often.

The world went topsy-turvy when the London office of Smith, LLC ceased to exist one Monday afternoon. A van that was expected to arrive from a painting contractor did arrive; it was waved into the inner courtyard and then blew up. Nearly sixty percent of the staff was killed. There was an additional ominous message: no one claimed responsibility for the disaster.

Smith, LLC clamped down and stopped all travel plans, and began notifying all of its personnel to operate in the shadows. The Smiths employed numerous resources to sift and twist the news and deflect it from them specifically to everyone else generically.

It was then discovered by Smith, LLC that as soon as the building in London had collapsed, the first set of rescue workers on the scene were in fact Church operatives. And they had gathered two survivors and two of the company computers. The very heart of Smith, LLC was presumably exposed, as the missing laptops were from senior staff members.

———————

Omak assembled his team in a desolate section of eastern Oregon. They all looked capable. They practiced with their firearms until they could shoot, reload, clear jams, and make the adjustment from close range shots to long range shots with alacrity. They began to function well as a team. Much time was spent going over the maps and satellite imagery that the Church provided them. To aid in their training, Omak converted an old barn into a stand-in for the Beys' house.

He gave each man a number, one through thirteen, preferring anonymity for his team over developing any sort of personal attachments. They practiced day and night for two weeks.

Omak used the computer sparingly and never mentioned anything to his handlers about who was doing what, how many were involved, or when they planned on eradicating the Beys. He shook his head, thinking that the Smiths had monitored all of his previous messages, and that their foreknowledge led to failures galore. This time would be different. This time he would succeed. Omak remembered participating in school and department teams for track, basketball, soccer, and more. He liked being on the podium; he liked winning. Omak wanted to win again.

At the last moment, before they loaded up a nondescript collection of cars and trucks, the Church operatives transmitted one final version of the latest aerial photos. There was a message attached to the file. When the review of the imagery was completed, the team got in the vehicles and drove down the dusty farming road. Omak was the last to leave. When the vehicles cleared the broken remains of the dilapidated gate that led to the barn, Omak opened the message.

The message contained a map and a picture of a youngish looking man. Omak was directed to pick this newcomer up in Portland before heading north on Interstate 5. He typed back, "No, no newcomers this late in the plan."

The message that was being typed in suddenly stopped and was overlaid by the odd old font Omak had seen before. "Not a team member. An observer only. Proceed." The screen went blank and the computer shut down. Omak slammed his fist against the dashboard of the old Volvo. Against his better judgment, Omak picked up this stranger, this newcomer, near the intersection of Sandy Boulevard and Interstate 205 near the airport in Portland.

The newcomer had flown in the day before, rented a car, and picked up three packages from a small mail forwarding outlet near the Rodeway Inn adjacent to the airport. In his hotel room, he used his phone to check in with the old man in Rome. As always, communication was brief. "Proceed," was the only reply he received. When traffic had died down and his neighbors in the hotel had turned in for the night, he opened the packages and began the last of his life's work for the Church.

Omak met the young man at the arranged time at the hotel entrance. He had a small duffel bag tucked under one arm and wore black. Omak still seethed at this change in his plans and refused to do anything other than unlock the door of the Volvo, allowing the newcomer to enter the car. He stepped on the gas and let the clutch run out before the man had closed the door. No greetings were exchanged. They caught up with their small convoy where Interstate 205 joined Interstate 5 north of Hazel Dell, a suburb north of Vancouver, Washington. The young man used his phone to text some messages and then stared out the window as the landscape slid by.

Out of the corner of his eye, Omak sized up his companion. He did not appear to be armed. His hands looked like those of someone who had never done any manual labor in his life, except maybe playing video games with college friends. The duffel bag rode between the man's legs and other than when placed in the Volvo was never touched again.

The convoy of four vehicles arrived at a wide spot in the road that passed by the lane that led to the Beys'. At this time of year, there were at least a dozen other cars and trucks parked in the same area. A few hundred yards through the forest was a stretch of river known for excellent steelhead fishing, a place frequented by many locals as well as international fishing aficionados. The men donned camouflage outdoor gear and put on backpacks. Some of them carried long tubes on their backs that easily passed as fly rod holders. They dispersed into the forest, taking different routes that would bring them to their assigned spots around the Bey compound.

Omak pointed at the newcomer and motioned that he should follow Omak. The man slung his duffel bag across his shoulder and dutifully followed along. His hand reached into his pocket and without Omak's knowledge tapped the screen on his phone.

On the other side of the world, an icon appeared on the old man's screen. He leaned forward and clicked on it. He laboriously typed a command using his mangled stumps. A section of wall slid back, revealing an array of scanners and radios. A few of these clicked on, and the man began listening to Lewis County, Washington, Fire District 7 radio communications. Another crackle of static filled the air, and the Lewis County Sheriff radio came to life; then the Washington State Patrol radio came on. The program that the young men in the adjacent room had created soon transmitted chatter from a dozen different emergency radio networks, and the air was filled with broadcasts of aid calls, barking dogs, illegal fireworks— the chaff humanity surrounds itself with on any given day. The old man sat back and listened to life half a world away.

Omak set himself into position, directing the young man to stay behind a large western red cedar whose limbs bent down and touched the ground. He glanced at his watch. At 10:15 a.m. exactly, he placed his earpiece in and turned on his radio. One by one, his fellow assault team members used old Morse code to sign in with their numbers. Omak had schooled them all in not using voice across the radio unless absolutely necessary. He glanced around and caught the eye of the newcomer. The man had put on some camo gear and was patiently watching Omak. Omak held his hand up and signaled the newcomer to stay put. The young man simply shook his head "no," and then he slipped into the brush off to Omak's right.

Palix stared at Omak for a moment, and was on the verge of saying something when his phone vibrated. He crawled to the other side of the big cedar and looked at the screen. There was a text message that said, "You will be forgiven." Palix then began to fade through the underbrush towards the large house two hundred yards away. Omak stared at the empty duffel bag and the slight movements of the underbrush where the man had disappeared. Gunfire to his left interrupted his brief moment of anger. "Action versus reaction," his father had taught him. Omak checked the safety on his AK assault rifle and moved through the brush.

Alone, Omak took the tearstained envelope from his pack and looked upon his wife and daughter.

Tex took command. Ravenna corralled Dr. Lucerne and Selah in the main part of the house. Ione, Neah, and Dreadlocks were out at one of the two caretaker houses, running some scenarios. Tall Guy drove up in the armored Suburban. He left the engine running and electrically opened the passenger doors. Dreadlocks unrolled his Kevlar blankets and threw them over Ione and Neah. He took out his small heat-seeking devices and, from inside, spent five minutes scanning the area. When satisfied, he opened the front door and shouted, "Go, get in the 'Burb and don't stop for nothing!" Running blindly with a heavy bullet-proof blanket was harder than Neah thought it would be.

Bey ran into the rear passenger door and tried to improve his looks by imprinting the door edge on his face. "Damn," he cursed. "That hurt!" Once Ione, Bey, and Dreadlocks had all tumbled in, the doors of the 'Burb slammed closed and Tex threw gravel around the circular drive. Bey was still a little out of sorts, with a trickle of blood running down his chin.

Ione asked, "Just what the hell is going on here?" They had done little drills designed to familiarize themselves with basic security concepts. Bullets slammed into the glass on Ione's side of the 'Burb. Bey threw himself over the top of her, and Dreadlocks threw himself over the top of him. Ione did not appear to be amused by this in the least. Tall Guy twisted and turned the heavy vehicle around trees and through shrubs, and did a nice job of making a new crossing over the creek.

One of the design features of the house and the driveway was the wall at the house entrance. There were only a few places on the entire the property from which you could see the area between the front of the house and the spot where a vehicle would normally park. Ione called it the "funny wall," but it shielded that area admirably.

Tall Guy ground to a stop and they bailed out. Ricochets off the wall sent bullet fragments and stone chips over them, but they were not of a size or velocity to cause concern, not when bullets were flying.

Dreadlocks opened the double doors and blazed away at those areas with a sightline to the front entrance with an M16 that had a seventy-five round drum magazine. He purposefully stitched a line of destruction along the tree line as suppressive fire. Ione and Bey scrunched down and scampered under his fire. There was a loud crack from above, from a second story window, and the incoming fire ceased. Ione and Bey sprawled across the foyer floor. Dreadlocks slammed the doors just as a machine gun stitched a line of holes across the top of them. There was another crack from the second floor, and the incoming rounds stopped.

It was a brief respite. "Is everyone accounted for?" Tex bellowed from the top of the stairs.

Ravenna shouted from the front room. "I've got Selah and the doctor, all unharmed."

Tall Guy shouted from the foyer. "I've got Good Guy and Mrs. Good Guy, all unharmed. Dreadlocks isn't pushing up daisies, just yet." Dreadlocks gave Tall Guy the finger.

"Okay, everybody listen up. Hostiles are all around us. I've got a friend in the NSA who is going to download real-time spy satellite data to us in about seven minutes. Ravenna! Set up the dish and make the link. We need to know what we are up against."

Ravenna scuttled across the doorway between the foyer and the living room. She grabbed two heavy plastic cases and threw open the lids. "I'm on it!" Tex shifted his position in order to look out an upstairs window.

"Tall Guy, make a tour around the house, check the windows and all the doors."

Tall Guy started at the foyer and threw the two dead bolts in the front doors. "Got it!" He moved into the kitchen, making his rounds.

There was a slap of a bullet striking the upper part of the house, followed by a boom from the tree line. Tex shouted down again, "Dreadlocks! Corral and protect."

Dreadlocks shouted up, "Roger that!" He then turned his gaze towards Ione and Bey. "Okay kiddies, you stay right here while I collect Selah and the doctor, got it?" Ione and Bey nodded their acknowledgement. Dreadlocks slipped into the living room and spoke to Selah and the doctor. Shortly afterwards they all appeared at the entryway.

"Alright boys and girls, we are going upstairs to the middle bedroom, where we are going to wait this out."

"Oh, bullshit! Give me a gun!" said the doctor. "I haven't lived this long just to get pushed around by a guy who macramés his hair!"

Dreadlocks looked shocked. He took a bundle of his hair and looked at it and mouthed "Macramé?"

"Now, where's a twelve-gauge?"

Dreadlocks looked at the doctor, and then at Bey.

"Just do it, or we'll all regret it," Bey whispered. He checked his .45. Much to his surprise, Ione took a very nice SIG out of her handbag.

"Ravenna gave this to me when we were plinking last week. I meant to tell you. I wish it came in a different color, though."

Ravenna popped her head around the doorway and shouted up to Tex. "Spy satellite transmission coming in real time. I'm going to display and save as it comes in." She slid one of the cases around the corner. She angled a high-tech flat screen slightly backwards. Tex crept down the stairs; Tall Guy appeared from the rear hallway. They all gathered around the screen. The image was remarkable, except that it was of the entire state. As if on cue, the image centered on Western Washington, then on the central part of Western Washington. The focus picked up the south end of Tacoma, all of Olympia, and as far south as Centralia and Chehalis. In a few seconds, the screen displayed just the south part of Lewis and the northern part of Cowlitz County.

The image blurred for a second, and then the screen filled with the Beys' property—all the roads, the trails, and the trees. Tex whispered under his breath, "C'mon, don't fail me now, give me what I want." The image fluttered for a moment, and then shifted to a heat-sensing image. There was the house, the glow of the Suburban's engine, and more than a dozen figures forming a half circle at the forest edge.

"Yo, did we bake a cake big enough for this many?" Dreadlocks asked.

"I didn't think that they would attack in such numbers, ever." Tall Guy was eyeing the display.

"I don't give a damn how many that there are. Give me a gun!" the doctor insisted.

Selah put her hand on the doctor's shoulder. "Now, Doctor, we must maintain our composure and let these nice people do their job." Selah looked at Bey. "Even if it is half-assed."

Everyone looked at Bey, who said, "What? I'll bet I get a better reception with the crowd outside."

The Church operatives opened fire at the windows. "Then again, maybe not," said Bey, countering his own comment. All the windows in the house were bulletproof, but even so they had a failure point when struck too many times. Hunks of the thick glass and polymer showered onto the floor.

"Ravenna! Update the images! Tall Guy! Get to the CCT-Vs and report!" Tex looked around. "Damn and damn again. Dreadlocks, stay here in the foyer and watch the living room and hallways." There was a whoosh and explosion. The Suburban disintegrated. The bigger pieces of it were on fire.

Tall Guy shouted out from the den, "RPG, in case you are interested!" Tex looked back in the direction of his charges and fellow operatives.

Ravenna shouted, "It looks like three are down and out." Bey guessed it was time to act heroic. He kissed Ione on the cheek and looked over at Tex.

"I'll take the second floor with the Remington, and nibble about the edges."

Tex looked at Bey; his facial expression went from tense to amused to grateful. He really did not have to say, "I'll take any help I can get at this point."

So much for feeling heroic, Bey thought. He crawled off to the stairs.

When he was about halfway there, Selah grabbed his arm. "I'll spot your rounds, Stuffy."

Bey shook his head.

Selah stayed with him, squeezing harder to make her point. "In Herzegovina I spot for many snipers. I know what to do." Her grasp on Bey's forearm was impressive.

Bey nodded, "Okay!"

Tex bellowed, "On the count of three, a mad minute for Stuffy and Selah to get to the second floor."

Bey looked over his shoulder at the doctor and said, "Does everybody have to call me Stuffy? When did this happen?"

"One! Two! Three!" Everyone else who had a gun stuck it out a window or hole in the house and blazed away at the tree line while Selah and Bey sprinted up the stairs, splinters of wood and shards of bulletproof glass showering around them. Selah was very speedy, leaving Bey behind about halfway up the stairs.

Selah and Bey stooped over and made it to the upstairs office. Behind the two bookcases that were mounted on hidden hinges sat Bey's Remington, highly modified. It had a variable 3 x 30 scope with night vision capabilities. Bey was hoping to have this all wrapped up before dark. Selah grabbed a set of Celestron binoculars and a mirror. The mirror had a small counterweight and a clamp that secured it to any edge handy. She rolled over on her back and looked through the binoculars at the mirror's reflection of what was outside. Most people so arranged got nauseated in a brief period of time. Bey hoped Selah didn't.

"Target. Large white-barked tree." Bey eased the barrel up; just the tip of the muzzle was beyond the curtain. Bey took a piece of tape and stuck the flapping curtain to the top of the scope.

"Large white-barked tree would be an alder in these parts," Bey suggested politely.

Selah kicked the side of his calf. "Target one meter to right of large," she paused, "alder."

Bey slowly swung the heavy gun around. Just to the right of the alder there was a motion in the salal and Oregon grape. Bey could see a shoulder and a hand. The crosshairs settled where the chest would be, given the shoulder and hand as a reference. The target was covered by light underbrush. Bey steadied his breathing and slowly depressed the trigger with the fat pad of his index finger. The Remington bucked and there was a roar. It would take the 220-grain bullet less than a second to travel the distance to the tree line. Bey could not get the crosshairs back on target before the impact.

"A hit, a kill." Selah was cool, Bey admitted. She held steady when the Remington shot and watched the bullet strike the target through the binoculars.

———————

Palix got to the stone wall in front of the house; the tallest part of the house was less than thirty feet away. When he rounded the tree, and entered the scrub brush he lost sight of Omak until he seemed to materialize off to his left. If he saw him, Omak paid no attention to him. Palix had never been in combat before, had never heard a gunshot except in theaters or from a TV. Blasts from the house and the woods frightened him, chunks of sod were ripped up here and there, and fragments of stone or bullets struck at his torso. He watched, his eyes fixated on the horror of seeing one of his team members being decapitated by a rifle shot from the second floor. He had no gun, and would not have known how to use it anyway. Still, the weight around his chest seemed to comfort him, a holy armor at least in his mind.

———————

"Target. At base of third fence post to left of gate." She had spotted a person in full camo paint looking for them as they were looking for him. The Remington bucked, and shortly Selah spoke. "Head shot, a kill. Target. In woodshed, second window. Get on it! RPG!" Bey snapped the round off and prayed that the siding of the woodshed would not interfere with the bullet's lethality. As Bey shot he could see the ugly snout of the RPG pointing at the house.

The woodshed's roof exploded in a roar. "I did not see the shot to confirm the kill," whispered Selah.

Bey surveyed the smoking rubble of his prized woodshed. "Seriously?"

Selah patted his thigh, "Still, I think you got him."

Bey looked out at the woodshed. "Son of a bitch, I smashed my fingers three times hammering the siding on it," Bey exclaimed. Now it was a burning collection of loose boards and siding. Bey thought he would have to observe a higher level of safety when it came to the storage of thirty gallons of tractor fuel and chainsaw gas.

Suddenly, the RPG soared upwards through the smoke of the destroyed woodshed and passed out of view, blocked by the eaves of the house. Selah rolled to the door and shouted "Brace, brace, brace!" She then rolled back to her position near Bey. The grenade reached its maximum height and returned to earth, plowing into the small koi pond Ione had placed as the centerpiece for the back patio. It erupted in a fountain of ruined stone and water.

"Oh, that will make the little lady really mad," Bey said.

"Target." Selah punched him in the solar plexus, bending Bey over. The window frame and adjoining woodwork began to disintegrate in a hail of bullets. "We have been targeted."

"No kidding?" Bey muttered.

"We must move." Through the smoke from the woodshed, she had seen the muzzles of a couple of M16s swing their way. They crawled away awkwardly—the big Remington, scope, and bipod weighed in at nearly thirty pounds. Selah stuck the binoculars and spotting mirror into the back of her slacks. For a second, the round form of her buttocks was exposed. Bey flushed at his ungentlemanly stare.

Selah grabbed him and kissed his ear. "Idiot," she said, then bit down hard. Embarrassed, Bey turned his face away. They crawled to the top of the stairs and met Tall Guy there. Tall Guy glanced from Selah to Bey, not understanding exactly what he had just witnessed.

"CCTV shows most of the bad guys to the north, at the living room end of the house." Bey started to slither down the stairs. All that protected Ione from a dozen fanatics was a cranky old woman, a guy with a crew cut, a Russian gymnast, and a guy who macraméd his hair.

Tall Guy grabbed his ankle. "Whoa there, *hombre.*" At least *hombre* was better than Stuffy. "You have got to keep the bad guys pinned down with that cannon, or we invite an armed rush we can't hope to beat. Sorry, but you stay up here if we've got any chance at seeing tomorrow's dawn."

Bey squinted in Tall Guy's direction and said, "How poetic, asshole."

Selah crawled off to the low windows at the head of the hallway. Bey looked back down the stairs. Ione was nowhere to be seen. Even though it was Bey's job to carry out the Will of the United States of America, he was also a loyal married man. Tall Guy pulled on his leg again. "C'mon, Stuffy, it's what we get paid to do. I've got a wife and kids at home, and I am counting on you to help me see them again."

Bey nodded, and with one last glance down the stairs turned and crept down the hallway, settling in ten feet from Selah.

"Target." Selah whispered the location. Bang. "A kill." She searched the tree line again.

"Target." Bang. "A face shot. A kill. Target." There was an eruption of gunfire downstairs. There were several rapid bursts of small arms fire, and the intermittent thunder of a shotgun. It sounded like Dreadlocks' MP5 ended the barrage of firing. Then there was a most unsettling silence.

Omak watched as the Suburban came to a stop in front of the house. Parts of the wall shattered as impact after impact tore into it. From his vantage point, he could see people draped in blankets dart into the house. As the heavy front doors closed, the Suburban flew into hundreds of pieces as a grenade found its target. Black smoke obscured his view of the front of the house, so he crawled further to his left. The binoculars showed people running past windows and taking positions inside. Automatic weapons fire sounded from the entire perimeter of the tree line. From time to time, a roar would come from the second floor of the house and one of his team would fall in a red-tinged haze. The small outbuilding blew up in a fireball, scattering flaming debris outward over a dozen yards or more. A smoke trail followed a projectile as it shot skyward, lost speed, and then began tumbling back to earth. Omak stood, exposing himself to possible discovery. He hoped the explosive would strike the house and all would be over, but it fell short, into the back patio area.

Using the smoke from the burning Suburban and the destroyed woodshed, his team charged the house

Omak rounded the wall and drew his pair of Glocks with extended magazines, one in each hand. He blazed at the windows and doors as he ran up to the living room end of the house. Other team members were climbing through the remains of window frames when he saw the newcomer. He was standing at the point of the living room where two-thirds of the structure of the house was supported by columns. Calmly the newcomer pulled open his coat and revealed a bomb strapped to his torso. Omak turned and shouted "No!"

The newcomer disintegrated in an angry red flash. In a surreal moment, the expanding shock wave shattered the columns, bringing down the front of the house. Omak was thrown into the house through a split that had connected the front door through the living room windows to the collapsing columns to his right. Deafened by his proximity to the explosion, the house tumbled down around Omak, silently, in slow motion. Wood shards flew in every direction. Glass and plastic bulletproofing flew by, not making a sound. Omak could see bodies being thrown about inside. Some were the bodies of his team members. Some were not.

"No targets." Selah sighed. Bey looked over his shoulder and saw Tall Guy. He waved them to stay put. The front of the house had collapsed in a pressure wave of bright light, flying wood, and smoke. Everything from about ten feet beyond Tall Guy was a ruin of debris. That part of the house was once three stories tall, and now it was scarcely one. The setting sun illuminated the wreckage of what once was Ione and Bey's home. Bey shucked the Remington and pulled the .45 out of his waistband. Tall Guy threw a .45 automatic to Selah, and they dashed down the stairs, ready for bear.

It was worse than bear. Dreadlocks cradled the doctor in his arms. There were five dead operatives scattered amongst the wreckage and at various windows and doors.

"They rushed from everywhere. It was a shootout. Then the house exploded." Dreadlocks slowly rocked the doctor back and forth, as one would comfort a child.

Ione knelt at the doctor's side. "She jumped up and got in the way. She got shot instead of me." Tears streamed down Ione's face. Ravenna came forward with a first aid kit and started to place a compress dressing on the doctor's right shoulder and upper chest. Bubbles foamed from the ruined flesh. Tex motioned Tall Guy, Selah, and Bey to conduct a perimeter search. As they moved from places of concealment to exposed positions, no incoming fire greeted them.

They returned and gathered next to Dreadlocks and the doctor. Ione assisted Ravenna with the first aid efforts. Tall Guy spoke to Tex. "Nothing we can see, and I'll go check the CCTVs."

Selah walked away with Tall Guy. She said, "I'll get the night vision gear and check things out."

Bey knelt beside his wife. The doctor's eyes fluttered. She reached out a hand, and Ione took it. Dreadlocks gently rocked the doctor back and forth.

Ione looked back at Bey. "Is this bad?" He held Ione's other hand and nodded. They had stopped the foaming, but it still didn't look good. Ravenna looked towards Tex. "We need to get a chopper here and take her to Harborview right now."

Tex nodded his head. "Already done." As if on command, they heard the rotor wash of a helicopter in the distance. The chopper made a complete circle of the tree line, the FLIR unit on its nose swinging to and fro. Then it made a rapid descent and touched down near the ruined windows of the front room. Three of the largest men in the world scrambled off, loaded with gear.

"Okay, you stay put. You and you and you, back up. Now!" commanded one of the medical team. Dreadlocks continued to hold the doctor; Ravenna, Bey and lone gave ground. The doctor's blouse was torn open and one man placed heart monitors on her. Another inserted IV needles. The other man measured and monitored her blood pressure, pulse, and respirations. They began the dance of paramedics, calling out numbers and conditions, adding monitor pads, adjusting IV flow rates, injecting medicines, and placing the doctor in a shock suit. They came with a clamshell stretcher and loaded her on it. Two of the paramedics lifted her up and started to walk to the chopper. Weakly, she raised her hand and motioned them to stop.

"Is Stuffy doing any of the first aid?" she asked faintly.

Tex said, "No ma'am, he wanted to, but there wasn't enough room."

She dropped her arm and said, "Well then, at least I have a chance. Please don't let him shoot me in the foot."

She was carried off, and the chopper roared away to the north. Everyone turned and looked at Bey. "What?" he said.

Selah was about to say something when one of the injured Church operatives moaned. Ione turned and stepped forward.

———————

Omak was knocked senseless by flying debris. He lay still, listening to people who seemed to hover nearby, ghostlike apparitions in the smoke and haze. He heard them speak but did not understand any of what they said, as if he was watching a foreign film without sub-titles. He knew he had failed, and he moaned in anger and pain. A woman he knew from the operative pictures limped over to him through the rubble. Omak wanted water and someone to fix his leg, which was pinned in an awkward and unnatural position under him. He thought of Roslyn and Lacey. The woman pushed hair out of her eyes with a bloody hand, and with the other shot Delano "Del" Omak to death. His last images were of his wife and child. Those images turned to cold ash and burned his eyes shut. What was left of Delano "Del" Omak withered to a ruined nub of his essence. And from the center of that ruin, all that was left began to combust from within, for eternity.

———————

She knelt next to the man and asked, "Are you alright?"
The man moaned and said, "No, I need help."
Ione stood and then jacked a round into the chamber of the SIG. She shot the prone figure in one ankle, then the other, then in one knee, then the other, and so on until the

SIG was empty. Ione then jacked the slide back, pointed the gun at the now very dead operative, and pulled the trigger again. She repeated this until Bey got to her side and gently took the gun away from her.

"It's okay, hon, it's okay." It really wasn't okay, and never would be okay again.

———

Selah moved in with them after the house was rebuilt. Bey took a liking to her, as did Ione. Ione had to get five stitches in her left hand where a glass fragment had torn into her. The force of the blast had thrown her against the fireplace, injuring her knee. Tall Guy suffered several cracked ribs on the side nearest the explosion when the house fell down. He showed the Beys a picture of his wife and kids one day. Like the families of all Smith, LLC employees, they would never stand out in a crowd. Dreadlocks had to have an operation on his calf where he took a 9mm slug. Tex had a partial hearing loss in one ear but not to any degree that would impair his performance in the field. Ravenna was reassigned to rebuild the London operation. Bey smashed his fingers three more times putting the siding back on the woodshed.

Dr. Lucerne did not survive her injuries. Most of the team was there when she traveled over. The injuries, the distance to the trauma center, her advancing cancer, and her age all conspired against her. Near the end, she passed Ione a locket that she had worn around her neck on a thin silver chain. She waved good-bye to them all, and she slipped into a coma and died shortly after.

They scattered her ashes around her New England estate, at the Smith, LLC Caribbean island, and there at Heron Hall, as they renamed Ione and Neah's home. Smith, LLC managed to get a small vial of her ashes launched into permanent orbit around the earth along with some other spy stuff. She would have liked that.

They had a small service, attended by Selah, Bey, Ione, Dreadlocks with his cane, Tall Guy sitting in a wheelchair, and Tex standing at attention. Ravenna flew in on a charter from London. Shortly before they began, a convoy of heavily armored limousines pulled in. In addition to the thirty-person security umbrella, there were nine of the Smiths. That was more than any of the agents had ever seen together in one place.

Several of the Smiths and Selah made brief statements about the doctor, and that was that. One of the Smiths shook Ione's hand. As that Ms. Smith turned away, she looked back and said, "Welcome to the family, Ione."

They were winning, and only a few people, maybe less than a couple of dozen, knew the worth of their efforts. Bey walked by the basalt column he had tucked in by a stand of Western red cedars. It was unmarked. But it represented Dr. Chelan Lucerne, just the same. It would last thousands of years. Wind, rain, snow, sleet, and other natural phenomenon might slowly erode it, discolor it, and crack it. It, however, would last; it would endure, just like their efforts.

Ione, Selah, Dreadlocks, and Bey shared the little silver locket that contained a snippet of Dr. Chelan Lucerne's hair. Most of the time it sat in a small crystal container in a niche in the living room, where it was always sunny.

The old man was enraged with the news of Omak's and Palix's failure. He stood and struck the keyboard, the monitor, the desktop, anything within reach. Fresh wounds opened and blood laced the air. Grabbing the monitor with his one good hand and the bleeding stumps of the other, he threw it against the wall. Using his forearm, he cleared the desktop of its contents, sending the ashtray flying. Ash hung in the air, and an unfinished cigarette lay in the corner of the room, smoking. The hard drive in the computer began to buzz and hum as it failed. He reared back and kicked the unit across the room. The power cord snapped off, generating a trail of sparks that mixed in a surreal manner with the hovering ash cloud. The call button swung crazily at the end of thin wires. The robed figure stood before the door leading to the outer office where his staff had failed in their work, had failed the Church, had failed the Pope, and had failed *him*. The robed figure shuddered in anger and frustration. So much effort wasted. So much time wasted.

He did not go into the office; instead, he went into his private quarters. His quarters consisted of a single room, with a toilet at one end, a small sink, a hot plate, and a cot. There were no decorations, no crucifixes, no palm fronds—just bare walls. Two lights bulbs hung from cords that were laced across the ceiling from the few outlets the room contained; each had a string to turn the light on or off. A few hooks hung along the wall nearest the sink, and a spare robe and a towel hung from them. A bleeding hand reached out and took the towel; the other brought forth the wood rasp from a pocket inside the robe. Before he began his ritual penance, he pulled out a scrap of paper from the sleeve of the robe. He tore the paper that contained the names of Palix and Omak into small, red-smudged tatters. "No forgiveness," was all he said.

The espresso was nicely done, in small white cups served on white tableware. The café was on the Via Attilio Regolo, a little northeast of Vatican City. Neah sipped his drink and looked at his watch.

Ione stared without expression at the top of the Basilica di San Pietro. She glanced at Neah and said, "Well, I suppose it's time." She pulled a small makeup case from her purse. The case was decorated with what appeared to be mabe pearls, set in a semicircle. Ione pressed a few of them, and touched the locket around her neck.

Shortly, the espresso cups rattled on the tabletop. A column of dust rose from the nearby intersection as a large sinkhole began to develop. Sewage and water from large broken pipes began to fill the hole almost to street level.

It was thought that no one was injured in the collapse of the street. Such collapses of ageing infrastructure were not unknown in Rome. However, after many days of digging, shoring, and repair, five bodies were pulled from the crater.

Russell H. Ford

Russell was born; he wrote this book. Stop procrastinating and buy it. If you don't, well, people will question your orientation, political leanings, parentage, upbringing, social stature, cooking abilities and whether you are just plain fit to be on planet earth with the clever, witty, charming and sophisticated people that did buy the book. I am merely stating the obvious. Does anyone really read this stuff? Send fifteen dollars to the Russell Ford Society for the General Improvement of Russell Fords everywhere. Don't delay! There is a tremendous need that only you can fill! Think of the good you will do for me; that in itself should make you feel really terrific about this magnificent gesture on your part. If you double the amount to an even 30 dollars, your deity will smile down upon you!

de-pop.com